"You'll come to love him."

"But what if—" Meg gazed into her coffee. "What happens if I find someone else to love first?"

"Margaret Jordan, you're one and twenty and haven't yet. What makes you think—" Sarah gasped and set down her cookie. "You have met someone else."

"No. That is—" Meg pushed back her chair and paced to the hearth. She shoved a few sticks onto the already merrily crackling fire. Her face felt as hot as the flames.

"Who? When? Where?" Sarah posed the single words like sharp cracks of a whip. "Tell me."

"It's nothing." Meg pressed her hands to her cheeks. "I only met him once, so I can't have any feelings for him. But there's something about his spirit. His eyes are warm, and he looks right at you like he's not trying to hide anything. He—intrigues me."

"Is this mysterious man handsome?" Sarah sounded like someone placating a child who talked about an imaginary playmate.

"Hmm." Meg closed her eyes and conjured an image of Colin's face. "I think some people would think so. He has very strong bones and beautiful green eyes and red hair."

"Ugh, red hair." Sarah made exaggerated shuddering noises. "That's a vulgar color."

"Yours is auburn." Meg laughed and faced her friend. "He's from Scotland."

Sarah dropped her cookie into her coffee. "The glassblower? Meg, you can't be serious about this!"

Award-winning author **LAURIE ALICE EAKES** has always loved books. When she ran out of available stories to entertain and encourage her, she began creating her own tales of love and adventure. In 2006 she celebrated the publication of her first hardcover novel. Much to her astonishment and delight, it won the National Readers Choice Award. Since then, she has sold eight more historical romances. A graduate of Asbury College and Seton Hill University, she lives in Texas with her husband and sundry animals.

Books by Laurie Alice Eakes

HEARTSONG PRESENTS
HP791—Better Than Gold

The Glassblower

Laurie Alice Eakes

Heartsong Presents

To my agent, who wouldn't let me give up.

A note from the Author:
I love to hear from my readers! You may correspond with me by writing:

Laurie Alice Eakes
Author Relations
PO Box 721
Uhrichsville, OH 44683

ISBN 978-1-60260-674-6

THE GLASSBLOWER

Our mission is to publish and distribute inspirational products offering exceptional value and biblical encouragement to the masses.

PRINTED IN THE U.S.A.

one

Children's laughter rang through the trees. Her heart leaping to the playful sound, Meg Jordan increased her pace.

She wanted to tell everyone about her school. In less than two months, she would open the doors of the old building, and every child in Salem County, New Jersey, could learn to read and write, not just those whose parents hired a governess or sent their offspring to boarding schools. Any child wishing to do so would sit before her while she instructed them on the alphabet and sums. If all went well, she would add lessons on the history of the United States of America. For years to come, children in her district of Salem County would enjoy an education. In time all young people could remain home while they learned, instead of being sent away from their families as she had been, despite her protests.

She would start her school, fulfill her promise to her dying mother, as long as her father didn't make her marry before she was ready to do so.

"Dear Lord, please let Father change his mind." Her voice rose above the hilarity of the children and sigh of smoke-laden breeze through the bare branches of oaks and conifers. "Please don't let Mr. Pyle ask for my hand. The children need me."

And she didn't like Joseph Pyle, owner of the farm next to her father's. He was young enough at three and thirty, the same age as the United States and only a dozen years older

5

than Meg. He was certainly handsome with his blond hair and blue eyes. His farm was prosperous. But his smile never reached his eyes, and he always took the most succulent slice of meat off the serving dish.

Meg laughed at herself for assessing a respected man on such flimsy details. Joseph Pyle would make a fine husband. She simply found her school more important to her than getting married. No fourteen-year-old daughter, the age Meg had been, should have to be away while her mother was ill, was dying....

She mustn't dwell on that. She should be hunting up whoever had dumped a load of soot in the middle of the one-room building. Without windows to the building and both glassworks and charcoal burners plentiful in the area, she could expect some soot to dirty the floor. This, however, was far more than a dusting of grime. This was a mound, as though someone had removed the grate beneath a glasshouse furnace and emptied the contents of the bin in the middle of her floor. Nonsensical mischief, plain and simple, but she didn't know how she was going to clean it or stop it from happening again, if someone was set on tomfoolery around the as yet unused building.

"I need windows," she declared aloud. "They can even be crown glass."

Most houses had crown glass. It was thick in the middle, and though one could only see clearly through it on the edges, it let in light and kept out the elements. It would keep out undesirable persons who sabotaged a mostly unused building, since she would be able to lock the door.

Ahead of her, the laughter of the young people shifted to yells and shrieks. Meg slowed. If the game they were playing was boisterous, she didn't want to charge into the midst of it.

She reached the bend in the road, where a lightning-struck pine leaned over the burbling creek like an old woman drawing water. The lane widened there with a narrow track leading to several small farms and the furnaces of the charcoal burners. In the midst of the Y-shaped intersection, half a dozen boys raced from corner to corner in pursuit of several kittens.

"You're herding cats?" Meg stopped to stare at the game.

If it was a game. It appeared more like chaos with each youth—from the youngest of perhaps five years to the eldest of somewhere around twelve—diving, ducking, and careening into one another as they charged after tiny balls of black-and-white fur. The felines also lacked a plan for their escape. They darted one way, lashed out needlelike claws to fend off a reaching hand, then sprang in the opposite direction. Boys yelled over scratches and laughed at cats somersaulting over one another.

"If you just stand still—"

Two boys no older than five or six streaked past her, jostling her to the edge of the road, and dove onto one of the kittens.

"Bring it here," an older child called.

Meg glanced his way and caught her breath. "No, you can't."

The boy held up a burlap bag that bulged and wriggled, proclaiming the cat now on its way to the sack was not going to be the first occupant.

"Let them go," Meg cried.

The boys swung toward her and froze. The still-free cats vanished from sight.

"Now look what you've done." The boy with the bag glared at Meg. "They're gettin' away."

"Of course they are." Meg stared right back at him. "Would you want someone to put you in a sack?"

"I'm not a cat." The youth of perhaps twelve years shook the bag.

A pitiful yowling rose from inside the rough fabric.

"Let them go." Meg threw back her shoulders—in an effort to make herself appear taller, more authoritative, more menacing if possible—and narrowed her eyes. "You must never harm an animal."

"But Pa said we was to get rid of them." One of the younger boys stuck out his lower lip. "We can't disobey Pa."

Meg winced. The child was right. If their father told them to do something, then they should do it. But stuffing kittens into a sack was unacceptable.

"Did he say how"—she swallowed—"you should get rid of them?"

"Nope." The eldest boy ground the toe of his clog into the sand. "He just gave us the bag of kittens and said to take 'em away."

"But Davy dropped the bag and they got away," another boy said.

"Then you should have left it at that." Meg crossed her arms. "Indeed, set the bag down and let the others go free."

"Can't," the eldest boy insisted. "It's too close to home, and they'll just go back."

"Pa says they're a menace," another youth piped up. "He tripped over one and burned his arm on the charcoal burner."

"Dear me." Meg tapped her foot.

From the corner of her eye, she caught movement in the lightning-struck tree. Gray wings blended into cloudy sky as a dove took flight. In response, a plaintive *ma–row* drifted from the branches.

Meg's heart sank. No doubt the kitten didn't know how to get down from the tree or would slip and fall into the foaming water. It was so tiny it couldn't possibly survive on its own.

None of them appeared old enough to survive on their own. Even if the boys let them go and the cats didn't get back home, they probably wouldn't live.

"All right." Meg took a deep breath. "Round up the kittens, and I'll take them to my father's farm. We have so many—"

The boys' shouts drowned out her claim that her father

wouldn't notice more cats in the barn or stable. Rough shoe-clad feet thumping and white paws flashing, boys and cats set up their game of tag. Meg watched, half amused, half concerned. Kittens scratched, and two of the boys cried out in protest then held up bleeding hands. Shortly, however, far faster than their earlier efforts, the children held all but one kitten inside the bag.

That bag pulsed and writhed in the eldest child's hand. The *me–ews* emanating from it were enough to break Meg's heart, and she began to wonder just how she was going to get the sack home.

"How will we get the last kitten?" the youngest boy asked, pointing to the lightning-shot pine.

Meg followed the direction of the jabbing finger and drew her brows together. The tiny cat still clung to a sturdy branch, well out over the rushing waters of the creek.

"One of you will have to climb up and get him?" The statement came out as a question and not as the suggestion she intended.

The children met it with blank faces and shakes of their identical blond heads.

"No, miss," the eldest one finally said. "Pa don't allow us to climb that tree."

"Father *doesn't* let you," Meg said, correcting his grammar.

"That's right, miss." The boy nodded. "He don't."

Meg tightened the corners of her mouth to keep herself from smiling at his impudence. But her amusement died with a plaintive *me–ew* from the tree.

"We can't leave him there." She sounded about as mournful as the cat. "Please—" She snapped her lips together.

She couldn't ask the boys to disobey their father. Nor could she let the kitten remain in the tree. It was so small an owl might get it after dark, or if it grew tired and fell, it would drown in the creek.

She glanced down at her muslin skirt. The gown was

an old one she'd worn to inspect the progress of the work on the school. She could do it little harm. And what was a gown or her dignity in comparison to the life of a cat?

"I suppose there's no help for it." She glanced at the boys, the eldest one still holding the sack. "Leave the kittens on the edge of the road and run along home."

At least they didn't need to watch her make a fool of herself, and the narrowness and remoteness of the road assured her no one else would come along to witness it either. The hour was still too early for one of the Jordan or Pyle farmworkers or men from her father's glassworks to travel home that way.

"You can assure your father the cats are gone."

"Yes, miss." The eldest youth drew the drawstring tight around the neck of the bag and laid it on the grassy verge of the road. Then, with shouts rather like victory cries, he raced up the track to the charcoal burners. His brothers followed. Just as they disappeared through the trees, the youngest one paused, turned back, and waved.

Meg waved back, thinking how much the children needed her school.

Yowls from the sack and a piteous squeal from the tree reminded her she'd better hurry if she intended to rescue the last kitten. First reassuring herself no one was coming along the road, she dropped her cloak next to the bag of kittens then drew the back of her skirt between her ankles up to the front and tucked it into the ribbon tied around the high waist of her gown. Shivering in the chilly October wind, she headed for the tree.

The pine was dead, seared by lightning from the previous summer. Most of the needles had long since swirled away down the stream, but the remaining branches appeared sturdy and close enough together for easy climbing. She simply hadn't climbed a tree since she and her dearest friend, Sarah, had been fourteen. They'd hidden from some boy who wanted to cut off their plaits. Meg had climbed plenty of trees before that day when she'd decided if she was old enough for boys to flirt with her, however roughly, she was too old for hoydenish antics. She supposed no one truly forgot how to climb, except she'd never climbed a tree leaning precariously over foaming water and sharp rocks.

"Please don't let me fall." She sent up a murmured prayer and stepped on the lowest branch she could reach.

The limb held firm. It didn't even bow under her slight weight. She caught hold of higher branches and drew herself up another level. Despite appearing as though it would tumble into the creek with the first winter storm, the tree remained strong. Half a dozen more sets of limbs took her over the water. It bubbled and splashed, sending up white plumes where it broke at the rocks. Meg's head spun, and she lifted her gaze to the kitten not more than a yard away.

The poor creature clung with paws no bigger than her pinky fingernail. Its emerald green eyes took up half of its face, and its pink mouth opened and closed in constant cries for help.

"I'm—coming, baby. Hang—"

Her foot slipped off the branch. She let out her own howl for aid.

"Hang on, lass, I'll be right there."

The voice, deep and masculine, slammed against Meg's ears like a blow, and she jumped, losing her grip with one hand. She glanced to the road to make certain she wasn't hearing things. Unfortunately she wasn't. A man sprinted around the bend in the lane, long legs making short work of the distance, bright hair glowing like a sunset.

Meg wondered what would happen if she let herself fall into the creek. She supposed she'd be badly hurt instead of merely sinking far enough into the water to swim away and come up out of the man's sight.

"All for a silly kitten," she grumbled.

"Ma–row?" that silly kitten responded.

Meg narrowed her eyes to glare at him. She may as well rescue him. If she couldn't go down, down, down into the water, she may as well go up, up, up to the cat.

She reached up and grasped the next higher branch. Her left foot snagged near the trunk of the tree. She raised her right foot for the next stair-step limb.

"Do not—" the man called.

Too late. Meg stepped onto the branch. A crack like a rifle shot echoed through the trees, and the limb gave way.

two

Nothing but thin air lay between Meg's right foot and the creek twenty feet below. Her left foot began to slip.

"Ahh—ahh—ahh!" she shrieked.

Nubs of pine needles dug into her palms. Her arms ached with the strain of keeping herself from falling.

"Hold on, lass, I'm here now."

And he was. A firm hand grasped her right foot, set it on a sturdy toehold, then repeated the process with the left.

"You can move your left hand to the lower branch, can you now?"

With him so close to her, she noticed his accent, a rolling burr of the *r*'s and musical cadence. She wondered who he was. She hadn't heard of any newcomers.

How mortifying to have a stranger see her in such an ignominious position. Nearly as embarrassing as having someone she knew see her acting in so unwomanly a manner.

"Are you too frightened to move then?" The man's tone was gentle. "Come now, it's not so far down."

It sounded like "doon."

"Lass?" He tapped her foot.

Her foot was encased in a sturdy leather boot but was far too exposed with her skirt kilted up into her sash. Her stomach felt as though it dropped into those boots. Her face burned despite the cold. Perhaps if she scrambled down the tree, she could run off before he discovered her identity. The deep brim of her hat should obscure her features from his position behind and below her.

"Let go of the branch with your left hand." The command was firm but calm. "Place it on the branch below it."

The kitten yowled.

Meg managed to release her left hand from the limb and reach for the little creature. With her feet now on a lower branch, she fell far short of the feline. Her outstretched hand flailed in the air. She teetered on her perch.

"Do not tumble into the burn, lass," the man admonished her. "I doubt I can catch you. Just grab the branch below where your right hand is."

"But the kitten. . ." At last she managed a squeaky explanation.

"Do not fash yourself about the wee beastie. I'll fetch her down. But first I must get you on the ground."

"All right then." Meg took a deep, steadying breath.

The faster she got down, the faster she could get herself away from this stranger who was seeing her ankles. Even if her boots covered those ankles, for anyone to see the tops of her boots was improper.

"I can do it," she added.

"I have no doubt of it."

With the cat staring at her with wide, accusing eyes, Meg curled the fingers of her left hand around the lower branch. She managed to release the grip of her right hand enough to move it below. Her balance improved at once, and she made the slanting descent with ease and speed if not grace. Always she knew the stranger moved ahead of her, watching her, ready to steady her if she slipped again.

By the time she attained the ground, her heart beat so hard she could scarcely breathe. Her hands shook as she tugged her skirt free from her sash, her legs trembled, and she hugged herself against the cold blast of the wind and to stop the shivers coursing through her body.

"Your cloak?" He picked up the garment and draped it around her shoulders.

"Thank you." She caught hold of the collar before he let go.

Their fingers grazed, and a shiver different than those

produced by the cold air raced through her. She looked up to his face, more than a head above hers, and her mouth went dry.

He had the greenest eyes she'd ever seen—eyes as green as grass before the summer heat turned it brown. Eyes as green as the emerald in her mother's betrothal ring but much warmer. Eyes as green as the kittens', though certainly not frightened. The thought made her smile.

He smiled in return. "There now, was that so bad?"

"Yes." She glanced toward the tree and up to where she'd dangled. "Quite dreadful."

The man laughed. "Then you're a braw lass to climb a half-dead tree after a wee kitten." He glanced at the more subdued but still squirming bag of cats. "You were rescuing them, I presume?"

"Certainly." She stiffened. "Did you think I risked my life so I could toss them into the creek?"

"Nay, lass, nothing so unkind." His fair skin tinged a fiery red that clashed with his hair. "I'll be fetching the wee thing down."

He swung around and climbed the tree with the agility of a feline. In moments he was reaching his hand toward the kitten. The ungrateful little beast darted away, dug its claws into the trunk, and streaked to the ground.

Meg snatched it up and hastened for the sack of its relatives. The others protested and writhed, jabbing claws through the sacking and setting up a caterwauling loud enough to be heard across Delaware Bay. She could scarcely hold on to her burden.

"Allow me." The stranger appeared beside her, holding out a broad, long-fingered hand with several white scars crisscrossing the back of it. "I'll take care of the wee thing."

"Thank you." She relinquished the kitten into his hold. The tiny feline nestled into the palm of his hand, and he stroked its soft fur with a forefinger before lifting the burlap bag and tucking the kitten into the mouth.

"They don't much like it." He cradled the bag in the crook of his arm. "I can carry it for you if you don't have far to go."

"No, not far." Meg lowered her gaze to the toes of her boots and gestured down the road. "It's no more than half a mile."

"Then, if you'll give me a moment to fetch my bag, I'll accompany you. I'm heading that way as well."

"I'd best not."

Father didn't care so much if she walked the half mile to the school building on her own, but if she returned home in the company of a stranger—a male stranger—Father would likely insist she go nowhere without someone accompanying her. That was never a difficulty when her friend Sarah was well, though once Sarah married, she would be too occupied with her husband to join Meg in her projects, and Meg didn't want to be thwarted because Father placed restrictions on her movements.

"I don't think I should." She glanced up the track toward the charcoal burners, wondering if she dared cut through the trees to her house. "I can manage."

"Perhaps you can, but—ah." He grinned. "I beg your pardon. I am forgetting my manners." He set down the bag and removed the small round cap from his head. "My name is Colin Grassick, newly arrived in New Jersey from Edinburgh—Scotland."

"How do you do?" She bobbed a curtsy and posed a question so he wouldn't notice she had no intention of giving him her name—so he could tell no one he had rescued Miss Jordan from a tree. "What brings you so far from home?"

"My profession." He indicated the leather bag he carried, which was at least a yard long and clanked metallically.

"Your profession?"

Meg feared she sounded astounded, but he didn't look like a professional man. He wore simple dark wool breeches and worsted stockings, brogans, and a plain wool jacket. Doctors and lawyers wore finer suits and top hats; light, leather shoes with buckles; and showed snowy shirts with cravats. Maybe they did things differently in Scotland. She hoped so—not that what he did for a living made any difference to her.

He gave her a gentle smile as though understanding what she was thinking of his appearance. Or maybe she was staring too long.

"I'm a glassblower," he told her.

She gave him an overly bright smile to mask the unreasonable stab of disappointment in her middle. "Then I assume you're heading for the Jordan glassworks?"

"Aye, that I am." His face lit as though the prospect of working in the hot, noisome glassworks made him happy. "Shall I carry the kittens until our paths part?"

"Thank you." She nodded then set out along the road, telling herself he wouldn't find out anything. The glassworks came before the entrance to the farm.

He fell into step beside her, hefting his bag of tools and the sack of kittens, the latter squalling with every step. He didn't say anything, and she strove for a conversational gambit. Walking beside a stranger, one doing her a favor, without speaking felt uncomfortable.

"No one's mentioned Mr. Jordan hired another glassblower," she blurted out.

"I expect no one thought it important to you." His long legs set a fast pace for her to keep up with. "Ladies don't usually take an interest in business matters."

"Not usually, no." She pattered along beside him as they stepped beneath the trees. "But we don't get a lot of newcomers here, especially not ones from Great Britain. Are you meeting Mr. Jordan at the glassworks?"

"Aye, he told me to come straightaway for the introductions and to get the key to my room."

"Room?" Meg couldn't stop herself from letting out a

breathless laugh. "Mr. Grassick, you get a whole cottage if you're a master glassblower."

"Truly?" He slowed and gazed down at her. "I never expected so much."

"It's the only way Fa—Mr. Jordan can lure qualified glassmakers here, providing them with housing big enough for a family." She peeked at him from beneath her hat brim. "Do you have a family coming?"

"If all works out here, aye." He gazed up at the bare branches of the oaks stretching above them, thick enough with the accompanying pines to darken the lane in broad daylight. "My mother and the bairns."

"You have children?"

He hadn't mentioned a wife, just his mother.

"Nay, my younger brothers and sisters."

"How young?" Meg's tone grew excited. "Young enough for school?"

"Aye. Five of them."

"Five pupils for my school." Meg let out a contented sigh.

"A school?" He stopped in the middle of the road. "The sort any bairns can attend? I mean—" His face colored.

Meg smiled. "Yes, a school for all children. At least I will soon."

"Seems an odd thing for a young lady to do." He resumed walking too quickly again.

"Not for me." Meg nearly skipped to keep up with him. "Father asked me what gift I would like for Christmas last year, and I told him I wanted to open a school for the children who don't have the means or time to go to the city for boarding school. There are quite a lot of them, like the boys who had the kittens. So he gave me permission to clean out an old, abandoned cottage and repair it a bit, so I can teach there. It's taken awhile, but soon the children can at least learn to read and write. Maybe it'll help them get a trade. We have so much need for skilled craftsmen here in America, but we don't have many schools out here in the countryside." She stopped walking at the end of a lane guarded by wooden gates. "This is the glassworks. If you pull that rope by the gate, someone will let you in."

"Thank you." He looked toward the gates but didn't make any move toward them. "Can you manage the kittens, then?"

"Yes, I don't have much farther to go."

"I'd be that pleased to carry them to your destination for you." He didn't look at her.

She kept her gaze on the road and building beyond the gates, certain someone stood before the glassworks door returning their regard. Her nose tickled with the strong scent of charcoal from the chimneys sending smoke from the great furnaces into the cloudy sky. She'd love to keep his company a bit longer, love to have more time to learn about his family and why he came all the way to America when the United States and Britain weren't getting along all that well. But if she let him walk her home, he would know who she was.

"Thank you, but you've done quite enough for me already, and you mustn't keep Mr. Jordan waiting."

"True, but I'd be that honored to serve you."

"Serve me?" She laughed. "I feel like I should be doing something wonderful for you. Your coming is such an answer to prayer for me. I can't open the school until I have glass in the windows. It's simply too cold."

"Does Mr. Jordan not have the window glassmakers already?" He glanced at her, his arched brows drawn together.

"He has window glassmakers and men who make drinking glasses. But people want more and more glass for their windows, and with the embargo last year, not much is getting imported from England or France." She wrinkled her nose. "Mr. Jordan says he'd give me the glass, but he needs to fulfill orders from paying customers first."

"Aye, 'tis the way of businessmen." He handed her the

sack of now-quiet kittens. "Someone's coming to the gate now, so I'd best go in. Perhaps we will meet again." With a courtly bow, he headed for the gate.

Meg trotted off before anyone from the glassworks reached the gate and recognized her. Once headed up the drive to the Jordan farm, with majestic oaks and pines keeping her out of sight from the road, she began to skip—for about ten steps. The kittens set up such a commotion she had to slow to a sedate walk. Her heart, however, felt as though it skipped along ahead of her, and she clamped her lips together to stop from singing.

She couldn't wait to tell Sarah about meeting Colin Grassick. Besides his being the most interesting man she'd met in too long to remember, he was also another glassmaker who would surely get the window glass done now. And he had brothers and sisters for her school. And she had more kittens for the stable and barns. And—and—

She skidded to a halt halfway between house and stable. Her heart dropped to the pit of her belly, and she heaved a huge sigh.

Father wasn't about to let her make friends with one of the glassblowers, let alone one from Great Britain. He might be willing to hire a Scotsman for his skill, but he'd not let an employee befriend his daughter. He thought it unseemly for a worker to fraternize with his employer. It might give the man notions of slacking off in his duties. So even less would he like the man talking to Miss Meg Jordan.

Had she been ten years younger, Meg thought she would have stamped her foot in frustration. This was America. Weren't men all to be equal? And surely Colin Grassick was special. Father must be paying him a great deal to come all this way. A skilled craftsman was far different from just anyone.

Resuming her walk to the stable, she resolved to talk more with Mr. Grassick.

three

She had the bonniest eyes Colin had ever seen. He held the memory of them as he tugged the rope by the gates and a tuneless bell clanged a hundred yards away. They were wide, round eyes of a golden brown hue like the finest amber glass, framed in extraordinary black lashes. He could gaze into those eyes for hours while listening to her sparkling voice.

If only he knew who she was so he could find her again.

He was smiling when a fair-haired man, in shirtsleeves despite the cold October day, pushed open the gate.

"Yes?" the man clipped out.

Until that moment Colin had forgotten to be anxious about beginning work at a new glasshouse in a strange country. Perhaps the Lord had sent the young lady along to distract him from his previous worries that the men might resent his arrival as a craftsman intended to produce the finer pieces Jordan wished to sell.

Inclining his head in greeting, Colin reminded himself he wasn't supposed to be anxious about anything. The Lord was supposed to take care of it all.

Except when His servants forgot to take care of their own, a little voice reminded Colin.

He swallowed before he could find his voice. "Colin Grassick reporting my arrival to Mr. Jordan."

"Grassick, am I ever glad to see you." The man's face lit up with a wide grin, and he thrust out a broad, scarred hand. "Thaddeus Dalbow at your service."

"My service?" Colin welcomed the man's firm handshake and warm greeting, but he wasn't certain how to proceed after such an effusive greeting. "You were expecting me then?"

He grimaced at such an absurd comment.

"Expecting your arrival?" Dalbow laughed and pushed the gate wider. "We've been praying for it. If you hadn't come now, we all would be trying to make the glassware for Mr. Jordan's daughter's wedding chest, among other fancy things."

"You don't already make the fancy things here?" Colin followed Dalbow into the tree-lined lane leading to the glassworks.

"Not often." Dalbow set a brisk pace past the tree line to where the lane opened into a yard stacked with charcoal.

The sharp scent of smoke and molten glass permeated the air, offensive to some, perfume to Colin.

"What do you make then?" he asked.

"Windows mostly. We've got a lot of need for windows, especially now that everyone wants just the clear glass." Dalbow grimaced. "Jordan finally hired an apprentice to do the cutting."

Colin understood that the man meant the process of cutting the thinner, clear glass away from the thick, gray, and nearly opaque glass from the center. He'd heard the French were working on a way to avoid that thick center altogether, using a process other than blowing and spinning the glass against a metal plate until it flattened out, but he didn't know if they were successful and never much liked making windows enough to care.

"Do you fit the pieces into the frames here then?" Colin glanced around, seeing no evidence of woodworking.

"No, they go to a carpenter in Salem City." Dalbow strode up to the door of a long brick building with two chimneys jutting into the sky. "You may wish to take your coat off. It's hot in here with both furnaces going."

"Aye, that it would be." Colin set down his tools with a *clink* of metal and took off his coat.

Removing it would also protect it from any flying sparks. A shirtsleeve he could afford to replace but not an entire coat.

Dalbow opened the door. Heat and the odors of hot iron and sodium blasted out with strength enough to taste. But the long room, brightly lit from several clear windows and the two great fires, lay quiet save for the *crackle* of the charcoal in the furnaces, the occasional *clank* of a metal tool set on one of the iron gratings, and sighing breaths of the two men on their stools engaged in spinning out the sheets of glass for windows.

"Mr. Jordan?" Thaddeus Dalbow called. "Grassick is finally here."

From a desk at one end of the factory, a tall, thin man with hair nearly the same dull gray as the center of the crown glass windows rose. Despite the heat he wore a coat and cravat, and Colin wished he hadn't removed his outer garment.

"I wasn't expecting you until tomorrow." Jordan smiled, drawing out crinkles at the corners of wide, dark brown eyes. "I'd heard you just got here this morning."

"Aye, sir." Colin strode forward as did Jordan, and they met behind one of the men perched on his bench, blowing gently and steadily into a long pipe, while the parison spun into a flat panel. "The ship docked in Philadelphia yesterday, and I found transport here straightaway."

"Good. Good." Jordan shook his hand. "With your country and France at war, I always worry about ships crossing the Atlantic."

"Not to mention the limited number of English ships allowed to come here," Dalbow added.

"I had to come on an American ship from the West Indies." Colin shuddered involuntarily. "Two extra weeks at sea was not much to my liking."

"That'll keep him here." Dalbow laughed.

"We hope so, if you are as good as my agent in Edinburgh

says you are." Jordan turned back toward his desk. "Let's talk about your work and your accommodations. But I don't expect you to get started until tomorrow unless you want to."

Colin felt his lungs expanding as though he were about to breathe life into the molten silica. "I'd like to begin, sir."

"Good." Jordan nodded. "A man eager to work. I like that." He gave Dalbow a pointed glance. "If you please, Thad? I did promise Margaret she would have her windows before the first snowfall. And we have to fulfill that order for the new town hall before she can have the glass."

"Yes, sir." Dalbow trotted to one of the workbenches.

Colin's stomach tightened. Margaret, the young lady's name. A fine, noble name. The name of a lass of whom Jordan must think highly, likely making her too high for him.

Not that he should even think in that direction after so short an acquaintance—or at all.

". . .if you like," Jordan was saying.

"I beg your pardon, sir?" Colin's neck heated from more than the fires. "I was distracted."

"I said you can work on windows for a day or two to get back into your work, if you like." Jordan's tone showed no impatience, but the corners of his mouth tightened.

Margaret could get her windows faster that way.

"I would like to, sir. Thank you."

"I'll show you your quarters now." Jordan moved around his desk and opened a rear door.

They exited to another yard, this one with small outbuildings filled, Colin presumed, with supplies, the sodium and lime and other elements necessary for making glass. Beyond a wooden fence lay half a dozen cottages: neat, wooden structures with small windows and gardens that would be fine in the summer. Trees shaded the houses, and a petite woman hung laundry outside one of them.

"I built these so I could bring in skilled craftsmen, and

they could bring their families." Jordan headed in the direction of an end cottage with two floors. "This one is big for a single man, but I understand you have a family."

"Aye, that I do."

And the cottage into which Jordan led him was twice the size of the croft his family lived in now.

"This is fine indeed," he added.

Though it was damp and dim, and holland cloth covered the furniture, it looked like a palace to Colin.

"You have a kitchen," Jordan explained, shoving open a door into a stone-floored room with a fireplace at one end. "But if you don't cook, Thad Dalbow's wife is good at it and happy to earn a few extra pennies making meals for you bachelors."

"I'll keep that in mind."

The tour continued for a few more minutes, then Jordan led the way back to the glassworks and stopped at his desk.

"My daughter is getting married in a few months," he explained. "I'd like her to have some fine glassware to take to her new home. On Monday you can start working on these." He pulled some sketches from a stack of papers on his desk.

They were for drinking goblets, objects that required skill and experience without being difficult.

"Aye, sir. How many and what color?"

"Purple. I have a good supply of manganese."

"That'll look grand on a dining table."

"I thought as much." Jordan smiled. "Now, if you'd like to work for the two hours left to the day, I'll have Thad show you where you'll be working and introduce you to your assistant."

Jordan wove his way past furnaces and workbenches, racks of finished glass plates, and stacks of charcoal fuel to where Thad was just finishing up the first stage of a window. Thad let his assistant, a youth of fifteen or so years, carry the panel to the lehr for its gradual cooling, and he turned his attention to Colin.

"Help him with everything he needs." Direction given, Jordan returned to his desk.

"He's a generous and fair employer." Dalbow jutted his chin in Jordan's direction. "Better than some of the other glasshouses. What's he have you working on?"

"Windows, to start with." Colin began to unpack his tools: the blowpipe, the tongs, various cutting tools. "Then I'm to make some goblets for his daughter. He wants them purple, but I'd rather be asking her what she wants for herself."

"Jordan doesn't like us talking to his precious daughter, but if you can persuade him to let you discuss the glassware with her, that's a fine idea." Dalbow grinned. "She's as strong-willed as she is pretty and kind, but you probably already figured that out."

"I beg your pardon?" Colin raised his brows. "How would I be knowing that?"

"You've met her." Now Dalbow was the one to look surprised. "At least you were talking to her outside the gate."

"I didn't ken she was Jordan's daughter." He felt a twist in his middle that she had avoided telling him of her parentage, after knowing he worked for her father. "She's a bonnie wee thing."

"The most eligible female in the county, now that Sarah Thompson is engaged. That is"—Dalbow grimaced—"as long as the interested party owns land. For any tradesman it's as much as his job is worth to speak to her without permission."

❧

"But I always help with dinner." Meg frowned at Ilse Weber, the housekeeper, wife to one of the glassblowers and surrogate mother to Meg since her mother's death seven years earlier. "No one expects you to cook and serve."

"It's what Mr. Jordan told me." Ilse spoke in a musical cadence, her lips curved in a perpetual and genuine smile.

"It's not trouble to let you be extra pretty for your guest." Her smile broadened. "Especially not when it's such a fine gentleman."

"Mr. Pyle." Meg's stomach felt as though she'd swallowed a lump of underbaked bread dough. "I'd rather you sat at the table and let me do all the work."

"Now, Miss Margaret." Ilse laughed. "Mr. Pyle is the most eligible bachelor in the county. He could be dining with any number of girls, but he comes here."

"Because his farm adjoins ours." Meg sighed. "He and Father want it to be the biggest farm in the county."

"You shouldn't talk to me about these things." Gently spoken, the scold nonetheless hit its mark.

Meg apologized immediately. "I'd better go change my gown."

Feet still dragging, she climbed the steps to her bedchamber on the second floor. It was one of five bedrooms and overlooked a garden on the side of the house away from the glassworks. Most of the time she didn't smell the smoke from the factory. Beyond the garden, her view gave her a vista of trees and fields, bare now after the harvest, and, seeming to protrude through the branches of a massive oak, one of Joseph Pyle's chimneys.

One of the chimneys. Unlike the Jordan house, which boasted four, Mr. Pyle's dwelling possessed seven, as he had even more rooms.

Meg thought having so many rooms for an unmarried man was silly. But she didn't want to be the lady who made the huge, nearly empty building a home. She wanted to get married, just not to him. Or anyone else she'd met since she'd been of courting age. The difficulty was, she'd known all the eligible men since she was a child. If they were her age, they'd pulled her hair and played games with her. If they were older, they seemed like her father's friends and just too dull.

Father, however, insisted she wed soon. He wanted

grandchildren before he was too old to enjoy them. He wanted a son.

Mr. Pyle made a perfect son. He turned to Father for guidance on business and other matters since his own parents died when he was Meg's age. A union between the two families, what was left of them, made sense even to Meg.

"But I want someone I choose." She spoke aloud as she drew a blue muslin gown over her head. "I want someone who will let me have my school and my cats and maybe a dog." She yanked tight the ties under her bust. "Please, Lord, don't let Father make me marry anyone I don't want to."

An image of the glassblower flashed through her mind, that strong-boned face with his frame of sunset red hair. He would let her keep her school.

He wasn't considered eligible—alas. She may as well greet the dinner guest.

With her dark hair brushed and pinned up so a few curls fell on either side of her face, she waited until she heard first Father arrive home then Mr. Pyle enter the front door a few minutes later. Then she waited for a few more minutes before making her descent to the parlor.

"Margaret, there you are at last." Father rose and came forward to lead her into the room. "You're looking well."

"Thank you." She smiled at her father and then Joseph Pyle.

He bowed and returned her affable expression, except for his eyes. They were so cold, like the bay on a clear January day: a lovely pale blue but not welcoming.

She couldn't help herself from comparing those icy azure eyes to eyes the color of spring grass. Eyes like emeralds with the warmth of a flame burning inside them. Eyes that belonged to a man who had stepped beyond the gates of the glassworks and, in belonging there, stepped out of her world, as her father and friends defined it.

She had to force her smile to remain on her lips.

"I concur with your father's assessment, Miss Jordan," Mr. Pyle said.

Meg repeated "Thank you," like a sailor's parrot. She didn't want to say she was pleased he could join them, as she knew she should. It seemed too close to lying.

"I believe dinner is ready," she said instead. "May I assist Ilse in bringing dishes to the table, Father?"

"No no, she can manage on her own." Father shook his head. "Joseph, why don't you escort Margaret into the dining room."

"With pleasure." Mr. Pyle strode forward and offered her his arm.

Meg rested the mere tips of her fingers against the crook of his elbow and allowed him to lead the way across the entryway and into the dining room. A fire blazed on the hearth, warming the chamber and reflecting in the ruby glasses on the table. Those glasses had come from England with her great-great-grandmother, who had sailed across the ocean to marry a man she had never met—a colonial at that—because her father had lost all his money. Meg wanted not to merely know but love the man she married.

She released Mr. Pyle's arm as soon as politeness allowed.

"This is so much nicer than dining alone." Mr. Pyle drew out Meg's chair. "I eat in the kitchen or at a table in the parlor more than in my dining room." He waited for Meg to seat herself, then he nudged the chair closer to the table before taking his own seat across from her and on her father's left.

"Company always makes a meal more pleasant." Father sat at the head of the table and nodded to Meg to direct dinner to be served.

She knew many of the wives and daughters of the successful farmers, the ones like her father and Joseph Pyle, who could afford servants rarely lifted a finger with meal preparation or serving. Perhaps because Ilse had taught Meg about running a household after she returned from boarding school, she didn't like the older woman waiting on her. She rang the bell then clasped her hands around the edge of the table in an effort to hold herself in place and not jump up to snatch serving bowls from the housekeeper the instant she pushed through the swinging door from kitchen to dining room.

The aromas of roast pork and vegetables wafted along with her. Across the table Mr. Pyle's eyes lit with pleasure, and he licked his lips.

"The pork is fresh, not cured," Meg told him. "And no one cooks it better than Ilse."

"Ach, child, you flatter me." Ilse blushed as she set the steaming dishes on the table. "I went ahead and carved the roast in the kitchen, Mr. Jordan. This is easier, ya?"

"Much, thank you." Father nodded his approval. "And bread rolls?"

"I am forgetting them." Coloring nearly as deep a red as the goblets, Ilse scurried from the room.

Meg bit her lip. The poor woman couldn't carry everything at once. But she tried. In her next entrance she balanced plates of bread rolls, butter, and fresh apple slices.

"That is everything until the sweet." She bobbed a curtsy and scurried from the room.

"Joseph," Father said, "do ask the blessing."

Mr. Pyle prayed a brief but sincere-sounding message of thanks for the food and company. Father passed the dishes to Mr. Pyle first then Meg, admonishing her about how little she ate.

"You were out for quite a while today, Margaret. You need to keep up your strength."

"This is—" Meg stopped arguing and took another spoonful of stewed carrots.

"So where were you out to today?" Mr. Pyle asked. "Visiting Miss Thompson?"

"No, Sarah is ill. I was visiting the school." She turned to Father. "Now that you have a new glassblower, will I get my windows? I'd like to be able to protect the school from vandals."

"Vandals?" Father and Mr. Pyle said together.

She nodded. "Someone dumped a load of soot in the middle of the floor."

"Disgraceful." Mr. Pyle scowled over a forkful of roasted potatoes glistening with butter. "I'll send two of my men over to clean it up for you."

"That's very thoughtful of you, Mr. Pyle." Instantly Meg warmed toward him. "But you needn't go to such trouble. I can clean it."

"Never. It's no trouble. They're laborers I keep on all winter, but they haven't much to do." He set down his fork with the food untouched. "But do, please, call me Joseph. We are such old friends that we needn't stand on formality."

"Well, um. . ." Meg glanced toward Father.

"I think it quite appropriate to use Christian names." Father gave them each a benevolent grin. "Considering you'll be married in the spring."

four

Meg buried her fingers in the pale pink velvet of Sarah's wedding dress. The plush fabric reminded her of the furry kittens she had rescued from the rowdy boys and who now lived in the stable, adopted by a motherly feline. And inevitably thoughts of the cats reminded Meg of Colin Grassick.

She'd seen him twice in the past week. Neither time had they been close enough to so much as exchange polite greetings. The first time she caught sight of him on the far side of the glassworks gate, he'd smiled then avoided her eyes. The second time she lifted her hand and waved. He'd nodded in response but hurried away to the door of the glasshouse.

"The new glassblower is a fast and skilled worker," Father had told her. "He'll get you your windows straightaway."

The joy of that knowledge fell under the shadow of her father's announcement that she would marry Joseph Pyle on April 28, the Saturday after Easter and at least a week before any planting would commence, even if the spring proved to be a warm one. She had sat at the table stunned into silence, her insides feeling punched and unable to accept food. She would rather go to bed without supper for a week, like a recalcitrant child, than comply with her father's wishes. She had never outright disobeyed him in her life. Reaching her majority at one and twenty changed none of that. He was her father, and she lived in his household. But she couldn't do it, simply could not marry that man.

Not when nothing more than the sight of the near stranger, the new glassblower, made her heart skip a beat or two.

"If you're going to cry all over my dress," Sarah said in a light tone, "I won't let you help me with the embroidery."

"I'm not crying." Meg blinked rapidly and dislodged a tear from her lashes. "Or not much."

"Don't you like the color?" Sarah's porcelain-perfect face glowed with amusement. "Perhaps I should be getting married in red to match my hair?"

Meg laughed. "You'd look a fright. This pink is perfect and so soft."

"So expensive." Sarah knit her brows as she bent toward the minute stitches of silver embroidery around the square neckline. "It came all the way from Paris. Daddy does spoil me."

Mr. Thompson could afford to spoil Sarah. He owned a large farm, as well as a lumber mill near the coast and most of the charcoal burners.

"He loves having a girl after four boys," Meg said with complete truth, "and he wants your wedding to stand out."

"I know." The crease between Sarah's auburn brows grew deeper. "It's just so ostentatious when most girls get married in their Sunday best. But don't think I'm ungrateful." Her head shot up, and she grinned. "I'll just have to have several parties to have an excuse to wear it."

"That's right, and you'll be going to Philadelphia with Peter several times a year."

"Then maybe Daddy should have brought me more fabric." Sarah giggled.

Meg smiled, but this special gown for Sarah's wedding to Peter Strawn no longer made her as happy as her friend. Side by side with Sarah, she set aside the sleeve she was hemming with nearly invisible stitches. "I need a rest, or I'll strain my eyes. Do you want me to make us some tea or coffee?"

"Coffee would be lovely if you have some of those cookies of Ilse's." Sarah knotted her thread. "But I'll come with you. You're right about straining our eyes. It's awfully gray today."

"It's been gray for a week." Meg led the way from the dining room, where they had spread the gown across the table, to the kitchen.

Ilse stood at the worktable grating sugar from a fat, conical loaf. Cinnamon permeated the kitchen air, and Meg and Sarah sighed with pleasure.

"You are like my children." Ilse laughed. "You want coffee and cookies, I know. I have just taken them from the oven and am now grating the sugar for your coffee. Miss Meg, you run out to the springhouse and fetch the cream, but take your cloak. It's raining." She turned to Sarah. "You should not have come out in this weather with you being sick so recently."

"It wasn't raining when I left." Sarah looked as chagrined as a scolded child. "I'll just have to stay until it stops."

"You certainly can't take your dress out in the rain." Meg snatched her cloak off a hook.

A blast of icy wind hit her the instant she opened the door. Her nostrils flared, picking up the sharpness of snow amid the faint odor of charcoal from the glassworks. Cold moisture struck her face and pinged off a metal bucket by the door.

"Sleet," she called out and slammed the door.

She dashed through the half frozen rain, grabbed a pitcher of cream from the springhouse, and ran back. Her feet and hands were numb by the time she slipped into the warmth of the kitchen.

"You might need to stay all night." Meg set the cream on the table. "It's awful out there."

"Maybe I should go home now." Sarah stood by the door to the dining room, her posture stiff. "I could leave my dress here so it doesn't get ruined."

"Of course you can leave it here. I'll put it in one of the spare rooms, but—" Sarah narrowed her eyes at her friend. "What's wrong?"

"It is my fault." Ilse twisted her hands in her apron. "I

didn't know you didn't tell Miss Sarah that you were getting married."

"Oh." Meg pressed her cold hands to her now hot cheeks. "I thought—I didn't think—Sarah, please don't be angry with me. You must understand—" She glanced at Ilse.

"You'd think you would tell me something so important." Sarah's lower lip quivered. "We've been friends since we were in the cradle."

"Yes, but. . ." Meg sighed. "Let's clear your gown off the table so we can have our snack in there by the fire."

Without a word Sarah spun on her heel and pushed through the swinging door.

In silence Meg prepared a tray with coffee, cream, and sugar, while Ilse stacked several cookies on a plate. Meg nodded her thanks and carried the tray into the dining room. Sarah had packed her gown and the special embroidery threads into its canvas bag and added wood to the fire.

"I am sorry," Ilse murmured as she set the plate on the table.

"It's all right." Meg gave the housekeeper a smile. "She's just hurt."

"No, I'm not hurt." Sarah yanked out a chair. "I'm angry."

"Of course you are." Meg spoke in a soothing tone. "Then you'll be hurt, then you'll laugh at yourself."

Sarah chuckled. "You know too much about me." She sat and reached for a cookie redolent of cinnamon and butter. "So why did you think I wouldn't be upset about your not telling me about your getting married?"

"Because I want it to go away." Meg dropped onto her chair and poured them both coffee, adding large dollops of cream and pinches of sugar to both cups. "I don't want to marry him."

"You don't want to marry Joseph?" Sarah's hazel eyes widened. "Why not? He's handsome. He's amazingly blessed in his farm, and he's nice. If I hadn't met Peter, I'd have set my cap for Joseph."

"His eyes are cold." Meg wrapped her hands around her coffee cup, savoring the warmth seeping through the china. "And what about the school? I can't bear the thought of other girls being away while their mothers are dying, as I was. And if I can get it started and popular in the county, even girls like I was can stay home."

"He'll let you teach the children for those reasons." Sarah laid her hand on Meg's arm. "It's honorable, generous work, and any man would be proud to have a wife doing something like that. Peter said he's happy to let me help you"—her cheeks grew pink—"until we have children, of course."

"I don't know if Joseph will feel that way." Meg sipped at her coffee, reveling in the heat going down her throat. "He kept talking about how he needs a wife to make his house beautiful."

"Does he mean new furnishings or just by your being in it?" Sarah grinned. "I'll say it's you he thinks will make the house beautiful and that he's smitten."

"Maybe, but he's never acted smitten. Father's just mentioned he thinks a match would be a fine idea." She sighed. "For all I know, he asked Joseph to marry me."

Sarah laughed. "I can't believe that. But about the school. Did you ask him if you could still teach? Have you told him how you feel about children having to go away to get educated?"

"No, I was too shocked when Father told me about the marriage."

But Joseph hadn't objected to the school when she'd talked about it, explained how she hoped that, eventually, children could get a good education and live at home. He'd offered to send men over to clean it up and had, in fact, done so. He'd even agreed not to announce their betrothal until after her school opened and had sent her a gift of oh-so-expensive cocoa.

"I probably am being silly." Meg reached for a cookie but

didn't eat it. "I just want to marry a man who makes me look at him like you do Peter, and who looks at me the same way. This just seems like—well, it seems like a business arrangement between my father and Joseph, not a love match."

"I'm sure he must love you though." Sarah gave Meg's arm a squeeze and returned to her coffee and cookies. "You're so pretty and kind and good at so many things."

"But he doesn't look at me like he loves me, and he talks to Father more than he does me. Besides that, I don't love him."

"You'll come to love him."

"But what if—" Meg gazed into her coffee. "What happens if I find someone else to love first?"

"Margaret Jordan, you're one and twenty and haven't yet. What makes you think—" Sarah gasped and set down her cookie. "You have met someone else."

"No. That is—" Meg pushed back her chair and paced to the hearth. She shoved a few sticks onto the already merrily crackling fire. Her face felt as hot as the flames.

"Who? When? Where?" Sarah posed the single words like sharp cracks of a whip. "Tell me."

"It's nothing." Meg pressed her hands to her cheeks. "I only met him once, so I can't have any feelings for him. But there's something about his spirit. His eyes are warm, and he looks right at you like he's not trying to hide anything. He—intrigues me."

"Is this mysterious man handsome?" Sarah sounded like someone placating a child who talked about an imaginary playmate.

"Hmm." Meg closed her eyes and conjured an image of Colin's face. "I think some people would think so. He has very strong bones and beautiful green eyes and red hair."

"Ugh, red hair." Sarah made exaggerated shuddering noises. "That's a vulgar color."

"Yours is auburn." Meg laughed and faced her friend. "He's from Scotland."

Sarah dropped her cookie into her coffee. "The glassblower? Meg, you can't be serious about this!"

"Of course I'm not. A body can't be serious after one meeting and two glances. I said he interests me." Meg squared her shoulders. "And if he interests me more than Joseph does, how can I commit my life to another man?"

"Because you can never commit your life to one of your father's workers." Sarah gave her head a shake violent enough to send a curl tumbling from its pin. "No one would approve."

"Why not?" Meg's jaw hardened. "This is America. Mr. Jefferson himself said that all men are created equal."

"That may be true," Sarah conceded, "but not everyone thinks that, including your father. You know he doesn't like you being friendly with the glassmakers."

"Yes, I know." Meg returned to the table, poured fresh coffee and cream into her cup, and pushed it to Sarah to replace the one now filled with a soggy cookie. "He says he doesn't want to create resentment amongst them by showing favoritism to one and not the other. And I wish I could disagree on that head. But he's a stranger here without any family, unlike all the other men. And I want to be friends with anyone I choose, so long as he's a Christian of course."

Sarah gave her a long, contemplative look. "But what if you end up liking someone as more than a friend? Could you choose between him and your father?"

Meg said nothing. It was a question she hoped never to have to answer.

❧

Colin packed the goblets in a nest of straw and lifted the box onto his shoulder. After two weeks of catching mere glimpses of Margaret Jordan, he must now meet with her face-to-face to get her approval of the goblets for her wedding chest. He would also give her the happy tidings that carpenters were installing the windows in her school that very day, windows he had created with his own craft.

The latter news made him smile. He could imagine her joy, the way her golden brown eyes would light with joy. The former report burdened him in a way that made no sense.

"You do not even ken the lass," he admonished himself. "And you've been warned off."

He had also been given permission to take the first few goblets he'd created to Miss Jordan for her approval. Perhaps he was happier about the opportunity than a brief encounter called for. Nevertheless, his footfalls felt as light as the breeze stirring the bare branches of the trees as he set out for the Jordans' house. Sunshine warmed his shoulders, and the air smelled pungent with fallen leaves and pine.

He made short work of the quarter-mile trek through the woods and arrived at the back door of a fine, big house built of brick and stone, with several sparkling windows on each floor. Beyond the green-painted door, a woman sang a psalm of praise in a high, clear soprano. A hundred feet away, a handful of horses stood in a paddock, munching hay and a few tufts of leftover grass, and outside the adjacent stable, several black-and-white kittens cavorted and tumbled under the supervision of a charcoal- and silver-striped tabby.

"You wee beasties look happy." He smiled at the felines then knocked on the back door.

The singing stopped. Footfalls tapped on the floor. The door opened, and Miss Margaret Jordan stood framed in the opening.

Colin caught his breath. He'd thought she was a bonnie lass in the gloom of a cloudy day. With sunlight brightening her porcelain-fine features and drawing deep red lights out of her dark curls, she was even prettier than he remembered. That she wore a white apron dusted with flour over a plain blue dress added to her charm.

"Good afternoon, Mr. Grassick." Her smile of greeting

seemed as bright as the sunlight. "How good of you to call."

"This isn't a call." He sounded curt and worked to soften his tone. "I've come by way of business."

"I see." Her gaze swept past him. "My father isn't here. I thought he was at the glassworks."

"He is. He sent me over with these." He shifted the box to both his hands, holding it in front of him like a shield. "They're for your approval."

"My approval?" Her eyes danced. "Then please come in. Would you like some coffee?"

"No thank you."

He thought the smell of it brewing fresh in the warm, sunny kitchen was fine, but he'd never cared for the taste.

She laughed. "What am I thinking, offering you coffee? You probably prefer tea. I do have a bit here. Father doesn't like it much. His father forbade them to have it in the house after the tea tax before the Revolution."

"Revolution, you call it?" He stepped over the threshold but went no farther.

No one else seemed to be around, and he thought being alone with her in an empty house was too improper.

"What do you call it?" She busied herself with a canister of tea, her back to him.

"The unpleasantness with America."

She laughed as he hoped she would, the bubbling notes as pure as the song she'd been singing before he knocked.

He set the box on the table. "Tell me if you like these— send word by way of Ilse or your father. I should be going."

He should be running was more like it.

"No need." She spooned tea into a china pot then crossed the kitchen to close the door. "Ilse is around the corner in the housekeeper's room doing some mending. She can hear every word."

Colin relaxed—a bit. "But I should not stay."

"Of course you should. If Father sent you here to show me something for my approval, then he expects you to take the message back to the glassworks."

"Aye, well, probably so." He began to extract a goblet from the straw. "They are of my making."

"What are they?" She left tea scattered about and dashed to his side.

The smell of yeast and apple blossoms rose from her, aromas of new life. A new life like the one he hoped to have here in New Jersey, a life he wouldn't have if he let himself be too friendly with this lady.

Someone else's lady.

He moved to the other side of the table. "They're glasses for you." He lifted a goblet from the straw and set it into her hands.

"Oh my." Cradling the goblet in her fingers as though it were no more substantial than soap bubbles, she turned toward the window and held the glass up to the light.

Sunshine glowed through the bowl of the glass and flashed and sparkled off the twirling stem, turning it into a shimmering amethyst. For several minutes she simply gazed at the piece, turning it, tilting it, holding it to her lips.

Colin had thought the piece still too plain, despite his enhancements to the original design. In Margaret Jordan's hands, it looked fit for a princess.

Yet she stood in silence for so long his mouth went dry and sweat prickled along his upper lip. Any moment now she would turn and thrust the glass at him, tell him to return it, and inform her father it was nothing she wanted on the grand dinner table she would have with her new husband, the man who owned the biggest house in the county.

She faced him all right, but she didn't thrust the goblet at him. She held it out, forcing him to remove it from her fingers, brushing her smooth skin as he did so.

"It's—spectacular." Awe made her voice husky. "I don't think our glasshouse has produced anything so beautiful. Is Father going to sell them in Philadelphia shops?"

"Not these." Colin gave her a quizzical glance. "These are for you."

"For me?" She frowned. "Why would I need purple goblets?"

"For your marriage."

"Oh, that." She waved her hand in a dismissive gesture. "What nonsense. Joseph Pyle has many fine glasses all made in France. Crystal glasses. He doesn't need me to bring more."

"Then you'll be telling Mr. Jordan that, not me."

Colin couldn't stop himself from continuing to stare at her. Never had he met a young lady who was so cavalier about her upcoming nuptials nor one who turned down a fine gift from her father.

"I do the work given to me." He added the last to keep the barrier between them.

"And how many did Father tell you to make?"

"A baker's dozen in the event one breaks in years to come."

"Hmm." She tapped a forefinger on her chin and gazed at the ceiling as though expecting to find some text written there.

She remained in that pose for several moments in which the crackling fire in the stove and the snip of scissors around the corner made the only interruptions.

Then she laughed. "Mr. Grassick, do please tell my father I would like these for my betrothal dinner party and so I will need two baker's dozen."

"I'm thinking that's not a good idea." Colin repacked the goblet in the straw. "It will take me weeks to make that many with all the other work we have to do."

"Oh, I do hope it does. Many weeks." Her eyes sparkled with mischief. "Maybe the end of January at the earliest?"

"Aye, it could take that long." Colin forced his gaze away from her alluring face.

She was up to some trick, and he wasn't certain he wanted to be involved. Yet Mr. Jordan had said to ask Margaret what she thought of the work before making more.

"If she doesn't like them," her father had said, "we can sell them with ease."

He hadn't given instructions about her reaction if she did like them. Colin would simply tell Mr. Jordan what his daughter said and work from that.

And with every goblet he formed on the end of his pipe, he would wonder why she wanted to postpone even the announcement of her betrothal. He would wish she wanted the work hastened. A lady promised to another man was far easier set from one's dreams than one who remained free.

Not that he was free to be even so much as dreaming about her, but no amount of determination had released his mind from her image. Now it would be even stronger. He had scent and touch to go along with the vision of amberbrown eyes and shining curls; fine, white skin and—

He snatched up the box. "I'd best be going."

"You won't stay for tea?" She gave him a coaxing smile. "It's the least I can do for your effort in bringing the glasses here for me to inspect. And for taking my message back to Father."

"'Tis my work for which I am well paid already." He knew he sounded brusque, but he needed to resist the temptation to stay, and pushing her away seemed like the best way to do so. "I need no extra favors. Good day to you, Miss Jordan." He offered her a bow over the box and exited the house faster than was probably polite.

Standing firm against her attractiveness though he might, he couldn't keep himself from stopping by the stable to admire the kittens. They had grown in the past two weeks. A pan of milk, so yellow it must have come from a goat, stood in the cool shade by the door, and all the cats wandered over to lap from it in the midst of their play.

One kitten perched on the edge of the trough, leaning precariously over the edge to scoop up water with its rough pink tongue. Colin wondered if the one on the trough was the wee beastie who'd scampered up the tree and nearly caused his first would-be rescuer to tumble into the burn.

Smiling he stroked the silky head with a forefinger.

"Good afternoon, you little scamp."

The cat purred and butted its head against his hand.

"Aye, you remember me then?" Colin smiled at another cat trying to grab his sibling's long tail. "Have a care with your perches in the future."

With a pat he turned to be on his way back to the glassworks. From the corner of his eye, he caught the glimpse of Margaret Jordan framed in the kitchen window. She was watching, her face alight with amusement. He touched his cap in acknowledgment of her presence, and she waved in response.

Colin resumed his walk—for about twenty feet. In those few paces he felt something latch onto the back of his boot. He stopped. He hadn't noticed any sort of vine or creeper on the path in which he could have caught his foot.

It was the kitten from the trough, tiny paws wrapped around the back of his ankle as though its few ounces could stop him from going away.

"You daft beast." He stooped and scooped up the kitten.

Purring, it nestled against his neck, warm and soft and smelling of hay. For a moment he considered keeping it. Only for a moment. It wasn't his cat to take, even if it had decided it wanted his company.

"Let's take you back." Resolute he marched back to the stable and deposited the cat among its clan—

The first time. In the next quarter hour he repeated the action three more times. The fourth time, footfalls pattered across the stable yard, and Miss Jordan took the kitten from his hands.

"Let me fetch a basket and some rags so you can take her home with you," she offered.

"Nay, I cannot have one of your cats."

"Why not?" Her gaze swept the horde of felines. "Do you think I'm likely to run out of them?"

"Nay, but—" He laughed. "If 'tis all right, some company would be fine in that great big cottage I have all to myself."

"Then come back inside and have your tea while I prepare the basket." She spun on her heel and marched to the house, apparently expecting him to follow.

Colin hesitated. With her holding the cat, nothing stopped him from going. Nothing stopped him from staying, either.

Nothing except good sense.

five

While Ilse served Mr. Grassick a cup of tea at the kitchen table, Meg fairly skipped up the steps to the linen press for clean rags then back down to the pantry for a covered basket. All the while, the kitten rode on her shoulder, purring and kneading its needlelike claws through the fabric of her dress. Meg rubbed her cheek against the kitten's soft fur and smiled into those emerald green eyes, so like the glassblower's.

Not just any glassblower, either. Meg had seen glasses and vases, serving bowls and candlesticks imported from the centuries-old glassworks in Europe, and the craftsmanship was fine. Thus far she had seen little produced in the Salem County works that came close to demonstrating not merely the skill but the artistry Colin Grassick's goblets exhibited. He possessed a gift, and a yearning in her heart told her to find out what made him so humble in accepting her awe and admiration. If she could persuade him to take his time with the tea, perhaps talk to him about a few other pieces Father intended for him to produce, she could learn what lay in her heart.

The idea returned a song to her lips. Before any notes spilled out, however, Sarah's warning cut through her joy. He was one of her father's workers. Father might not—probably wouldn't—approve of her befriending Colin Grassick. And she was supposed to marry another man.

"I don't see the harm in being friendly, kitten." Meg's spirit rebelled. "Father sent him here to get my approval for the goblets."

Her actions thus justified, she tucked the kitten into the

basket and returned to the kitchen with her now meowing burden.

"She isn't happy about being confined." Meg set the basket on the floor beside Colin's chair. "Perhaps she's lonely." He lifted the lid and poked a finger inside.

The mews ceased.

"Ach, she's a funny one." Ilse chuckled. "Would you like me to finish with the bread rolls, Miss Meg? They're ready for the oven."

"So they are." Meg glanced at the buns rising near the stove. "I forgot about them. If you stay a few minutes, Mr. Grassick, I'll send a few home with you."

"Nay, I have enough to carry with the wee beastie and the glass." He lifted his teacup. The delicate china looked like a toy in his hand, yet he held it with care. "But I thank you for your thoughtfulness."

"Leave the glass here." Meg slid the trays of rolls into the baking oven. "Unless you need them for matching the others."

"Nay, I have my drawings. And perhaps these would be safer here."

"Ya, I can tuck them on the top shelf of the pantry." Ilse snatched up the crate of glasses and carried it into the storage room off the kitchen.

Meg drew out a chair and joined Colin at the table. "I didn't notice you at church on Sunday." She tilted her head to one side. "Dare I ask if you go?"

"Aye, I go." He gave her a half smile. "I saw you in the front row. I was in the back."

She was in the family's private box pew with Father and Joseph, perched on cushions to keep them comfortable in the event the sermon lasted a long time. Colin had just reminded her that he had perched on a narrow bench with the other workers, uncomfortable with the shortest of talks.

It wasn't right. The Jordan pew was half empty most of the time.

"Did you enjoy the service anyway?" she ventured.

"He is a fine preacher." Colin set down his cup and pushed it a little away from him. "I missed worshipping at the kirk while aboard ship."

"Have you always gone to church?" Meg grasped the edge of the table. "That's what a kirk is, isn't it, a church?"

"Aye, that it is." He rose. "I went with my family every Sunday until I ran away from home when I was twelve."

Meg stared at him. "You ran away from home?"

"I did." He inclined his head, sending a wave of sunset red hair sliding across his brow.

"Why? I mean—" Meg's face heated. "Never you mind. It's none of my concern."

"I think it is." His voice held a roughness she hadn't noticed before now. "You and your father deserve to know the character of the man you employ. I ran off because I wanted to be a Lowland glassmaker instead of a Highland fisherman like my father. The next time I attended the kirk was two years ago when I went to the funeral of my father."

Raw pain clouded his brilliant eyes.

"I'm so sorry." Despite knowing how useless the words were, Meg didn't know what else to say.

She rose and looked into the oven to see if the rolls were browning too quickly or remaining too doughy. She kept her back to him, waiting for him to compose himself, have a moment to say whatever he chose. She wanted to know how his father died, but she had already probed for more than was appropriate.

"He drowned somewhere near the Hebrides." Colin's voice was soft once again, calm, as though he had spoken these words many times. "The water was rough, and he shouldn't have gone out alone, but his wife and bairns needed to eat, and he didn't have his one son along who was old enough to be of use. If I hadn't been wasting my silver—" He broke off on a sigh. "Thank you for the tea and the wee beastie. I must be on my way."

Before Meg could get the oven door closed, he was halfway outside.

But he hesitated on the threshold. "Your windows should be in your school by now, Miss Jordan. I was forgetting to tell you."

"That's wonderful." She straightened from the stove, allowing the door to shut with a metallic clang. "If you wait another two minutes, the rolls will be ready."

"Thank you, but I must be on my way."

"Yes, Grassick, you should be," Father said from behind them.

⁂

Meg counted the kittens lounging about in the feeble rays of the late autumn sun. Four. The adult cats rambled elsewhere, hunting or sleeping or keeping the horses company, but the kittens tended to remain near the door except for the one who had taken a fancy to Colin and now one more.

"Where did your brother or sister go?" she asked the felines as though they could answer.

They didn't even look at her.

"Yes, I know you had quite a mole feast this morning, but where is your brother? Or maybe sister?"

A foot scraped on the beaten earth of the stable yard, and a husky laugh rang out. "I think you need to ask in their language," Sarah said. "A specific series of meows."

She proceeded to meow in several different tones.

The kittens rose, stretched, and wandered into the stable.

"Maybe it's your accent," Meg suggested through her giggles.

"I'm afraid I said something rude." Sarah grinned after the departing felines. "Have you lost one?"

"I have. He was around this morning, but now he seems to have gone off somewhere, and I'm worried he's lost."

"Cats are quite resourceful, you know." Sarah linked her arm with Meg's. "But let's go hunt him down. He shouldn't be out after dark. Foxes can be a menace."

"And the owls. The kittens are so tiny still." Meg adjusted her hat brim so she could look up at her slightly taller friend. "But you came to visit for something more than a kitten hunt."

"I did. I want to go see the new windows in the school before this fine weather ends. Have you seen them yet?"

"I have. They're perfect."

After Father sent Colin back to the glassworks with enough ice in his voice to fill Delaware Bay, Meg had retreated to the school to nurse her humiliated spirit. The windows were far better than Meg suggested, nearly perfectly clear panes set into frames of four squares a window. Light spilled across the hard-packed earth floor, now clear of soot, thanks to Joseph's workers.

"Now all we need is a stove or grate so we don't all freeze, and something on which the students can sit."

"If we have a brazier," Sarah mused aloud, "the children can make do with blankets and slates on their laps."

"I'd rather they were comfortable."

Sarah patted her arm. "You want everyone more comfortable. But you know, the Lord didn't promise us that we wouldn't have to suffer a bit from time to time."

"No."

Meg thought about the suffering in Colin's voice, in his eyes when he talked of abandoning his family. If she possessed the power to do so, she would have removed that pain from his spirit. She could only pray for him, even if praying for him made her feel guilty for thinking of him at all. She should be thinking of Joseph and a future with him because her father wanted that life for her. She should be thinking about the children and helping them have better lives.

"I'm afraid they won't come if they're uncomfortable." Meg kicked a stick off the drive and scanned the area for signs of a black-and-white feline. "We don't need tables and chairs or desks. Simple benches would do."

"Maybe the church has some extra benches." Sarah wrinkled her nose as they turned onto the road, and the wind, tunneling through the lining trees, struck them in the face with the odors of the glassworks. "How do you bear it?"

"I don't notice it most of the time."

Or she tried not to notice, to think of what Colin would look like, blowpipe to his lips, the other end of the tube glowing with molten glass. Purple glass. Would he think of her as he created the twenty-six goblets for her betrothal party?

"You should see the wedding gift Father is giving me." This was a way she could talk about Colin and not give away her attraction to a man besides the one she was to marry. "Co—Mr. Grassick brought them by yesterday for my approval. He stayed a bit because one of the kittens took a liking to him, and I fixed up a basket so he could take it home. Then he told me a little bit more about his family, about his father dying and the children—" Her footfalls sped up. "But I was telling you about the goblets. They're magnificent. When I looked at one with the sun shining through it, I would have thought it was made of an amethyst, the color was so pure and clear. And the workmanship—what's wrong?"

Sarah had stopped and turned to face Meg. Concern radiated from Sarah's hazel eyes. "Did you like the glasses because of the artist, or did you like the artist because of the work?"

Meg blinked. "Did I—what do you mean? I'm talking about the fine workmanship. Mr. Grassick is a talented artisan."

"That's what everyone is saying." Sarah nodded, but her face was tight. "And now he's told you about being all alone here in America and having family back in Scotland."

"Yes, it's rather sad. He ran away from home when he was twelve—"

"Shh." Sarah pressed a gloved forefinger to Meg's lips. "I'm sure it is very sad. But, Meg, he's not a lost kitten you can pack up in your pocket and carry home to feed."

"No, but I can be kind to him."

"While betrothed to another man?"

"It's not official yet."

"It's what your father wants for you."

"But not what I want." Meg heaved a sigh. "Let's go look at the school and try to find the kitten."

"Yes, I'm forgetting how short the daylight is now." Sarah resumed walking.

At intervals one or the other of them called to the kitten, though Meg expected it would be in a field or the woods, hunting or trying to, rather than along the road. When they passed the glassworks, she didn't so much as glance in that direction. She wouldn't see him anyway. Father had told her Colin worked longer hours than any of the men. He also helped out the others and never complained.

"If he works out, he'll be worth every penny it cost me to get him here." Father had laughed at that, his annoyance at finding her chatting cozily with the glassblower diminishing. "I wish it was pennies it cost me instead of a whole lot of dollars."

She mustn't interfere with her father's making a profit from his business. She must be a good daughter. She'd promised to be a good daughter before Momma died. Promised in letters. To be a good daughter, she must do what she was told.

"You're frowning," Sarah said.

"I'm worrying about the kitten. He's so small."

They left the cover of trees and entered the broad intersection of road, charcoal burners lane, and creek. Meg's gaze strayed to the lightning-struck tree, and she caught a flash of movement in the branches.

"That little imp." Picking up her skirt, she raced for the tree. She wasn't mistaken. Twenty feet above the rushing waters of the stream perched a black-and-white kitten.

"I thought the one he took home was the one he rescued, but who can tell them apart?" She began to kilt up her skirt.

"Meg!" Sarah gasped. "Your ankles are showing."

Meg stared down at her stockings, visible above the ribbons tying her blue kid slippers around her ankles. "I forgot. I was wearing boots last time."

"Last time?" Sarah poked Meg in the ribs. "What are you forgetting to tell me?"

"I climbed the tree to rescue a kitten. In the end, he got himself down."

"And probably will this time, too. Now tell me what you meant about the last time you climbed the tree."

As they continued their walk to the school, Meg confessed the entire scene to her friend.

"I can't believe you kept that to yourself." Sarah laughed so hard she had tears in her eyes. "It was too bad of you to climb a tree with your skirt pulled up, even with boots on, but to end up hanging there like an apple—oh my, the picture."

"It was more embarrassing to have a stranger see me like that."

They rounded the curve in the road that led straight to the school building. Meg stopped talking to smile, anticipating Sarah's exclamation of delight when she saw the slanting afternoon sunlight glinting off the panes of glass in the new windows.

Both of them exclaimed, but it wasn't in pleasure. Sunlight glinted off glass, lots of glass. What looked like acres of glass strewed around the little building.

Every windowpane had been smashed.

six

Meg started to cry. She'd waited for months to get glass in the frames for her school, and now they lay in fragments on the ground. Gazing at the glittering shards, she felt as though her heart lay mixed in the shining horde.

"Who would do this?" Sarah slipped her arms around Meg and hugged her tightly. "It's simply terrible. Who wouldn't want a school?"

"I thought the soot was bad." Meg sniffled against Sarah's cloak. "But that wasn't expensive to clean up. This"—she straightened and waved her arm in the air—"will take forever to replace, if Father will replace it. Do you have a handkerchief?"

"Of course." Sarah produced a square of linen with a tatted edge.

Meg took it and wiped her eyes—and kept wiping. The tears wouldn't stop.

"How will I ever be able to open a school if it doesn't have windows?" She burst out sobbing again. "It's not as though I'm doing this for myself. I want to serve the Lord through helping the children around here learn to read and write and some history and. . .how can this happen?"

"Meg. Meg, calm yourself." Sarah patted Meg's back then wrapped one arm around her shoulders. "We'll work out something. I mean, if your father was willing to put windows in once, surely he will be willing again."

"It took months to get these."

"Yes, but now he has a new glassblower. You got them within two weeks of Mr. Grassick arriving."

"I know. It's just that he's already doing work for me,

making these—goblets—" Meg's voice caught in her throat.

Meg felt sick. Without another word, she turned on her heel and began trudging back toward home. She'd found a way to put off her wedding by convincing Father that she needed glasses enough for a betrothal party. He'd agreed, realizing it would be an opportunity to show off Colin's skill to the county and get orders for their own sets of glassware. Although she intended to use the glasses for such a party, and although they would be fine advertisement for Colin's skill, Meg knew they were an excuse to put off the announcement of the marriage. She wasn't being truly deceitful—or didn't think of it as such at the time. Now, however, she worried that her action was wrong and she was being punished for not being honest with her father.

"What should I do?" Meg spoke to the Lord, but said it aloud.

"Ask your father for more windows. Surely he won't blame you for this."

"No, he won't blame me. It's simply that—" Meg paused in the center of the road and stared at the clear blue sky. "We need to stop at the glassworks on our way back."

"You want to walk up to the gate and ring for admission?" Sarah sounded shocked and justifiably so. Although Meg had visited the glassworks many times to take Father dinner, she had never invited Sarah to go inside the stockade around the factory.

"Yes, we must go now." Meg set out at a trot.

Sarah skipped to catch up with Meg. "Can't this wait?"

"No, I have to talk to Father before—before any more work is done on the goblets."

"Why?"

"Because—" Meg looked down.

A tiny creature whizzed past her.

"The kitten." She dove after it, catching it before it

disappeared beneath a clump of shrubbery.

"Wanderer." She tucked him—or her—under her chin.

A purr twice the size of the cat rumbled from beneath a coating of thick fur.

"He's lovely." Sarah stroked the small head between the pointed black ears. "And he likes you."

"One of the cats took a liking to Mr. Grassick. Just wouldn't let him leave."

"Maybe Peter will let me have a cat. They're so useful in the kitchen and pantry."

"Father won't let me have one in the house, but they're happy in the stable. Except this one. He seems to like to wander off and get himself into trouble."

"Looking for you?" Sarah smiled. "And he's making you look happier, too."

"He makes me feel better."

But the sight of the glassworks gates brought the nausea clutching at her middle again. No help for it though. If she wanted to make up for her trick in postponing the official announcement of her betrothal, she must face up to what she'd done, sacrifice what she wanted with the delayed wedding plans for the sake of providing windows for her school. Telling Father in front of his workers would be far easier than telling him in private.

"It's rather smelly in there," Meg pointed out. "If you'd rather go home, I understand."

"I'll come with you. I admit I'm curious."

"They may not let us in." Meg tugged on the bell rope.

A *clang* rang across the yard. Mr. Weber, wearing a leather apron over his clothes, poked his head out of the factory door. Meg waved to him. Even from the distance to the gate, Meg saw his eyes widen. He nodded and vanished back inside the building.

A moment later Father strode into the yard. "Is something wrong, Margaret?"

"No. I mean, yes." Meg put the kitten into the pocket of

her cloak. "May I come in and talk to you?"

"It can't wait until I return home tonight?"

Meg shook her head.

"This is no place for a young lady." Father frowned. His gaze fell on Sarah, and he smoothed out his brow. "I beg your pardon, Sarah. How are you doing?"

"Well, thank you." Sarah smiled. "But, if you please, Mr. Jordan, will you allow us to come in? I admit I'm fascinated by the idea of glass."

"All right, but only from the doorway." Father unlatched the gate and pushed it open. "It's not safe inside. We have apprentices running around with molten glass and men working on pieces. It's quite—Margaret, you've been crying."

Meg dabbed at her streaked face with the edge of her cloak. "Yes, sir."

"What happened?" He took her arm with one hand and held out the other to Sarah.

"Someone broke my windows. The ones for the school." Fresh tears stung her eyes.

Father's hand tightened on her arm for a second. "How—dare—anyone?" He ground the words through his teeth. "You didn't see anyone about? It was all right yesterday."

"It was perfect yesterday." One tear rolled down Meg's cheek. "I was so pleased. At last I could keep my promise to Momma."

"We didn't see anyone or anything." Sarah answered his question. "Maybe those rough boys from the charcoal burners."

"I helped them get rid of their cats," Meg protested. "And they'll benefit from the school. Why would they harm it?"

"Maybe they don't want the school." Sarah spoke her suggestion with hesitancy.

"No one will make them come." Meg found herself scowling at the still-open door, caught movement from beyond the threshold, and smoothed out her face.

Not until they stepped into the heat and smell did she

think of what were surely her red-rimmed eyes and tear-streaked cheeks for everyone there to see. For one man in particular to see.

She glanced around, seeking him out. If not for his red hair, she would have missed him on the other side of one of the great furnaces. He was knocking pieces of excess glass off the bottom of a finished work that appeared to be some sort of serving dish like a soup tureen. The glass shone like amber in the firelight.

"Beautiful," Sarah murmured.

Meg started, rather shocked that Sarah would make such a comment about a man. Then, face flushing, she realized her friend meant the glassware—not Colin.

"Shall we go to your desk, Father?" Meg turned her back on him in pursuit of her father's corner of the factory.

"Yes, just have a care. There's cullet all over the floor." Father picked his way over the flagstones strewed with chunks of glass that had been cut or broken from pieces.

Those shards would be reheated with batches of silica to make more glass. They wasted as little as possible.

Father's desk resided below a broad window formed of eight panes of glass. The afternoon sun blazed through the nearly clear windows and across an open ledger. He slammed that shut and indicated that Meg and Sarah should take the two chairs across from him.

"I'm not in the habit of entertaining ladies here." Father glared at someone behind Meg.

She tilted her head to adjust her hat and saw a young apprentice scurrying away.

"Yes." Father's smile was tight. "It's to keep the men's attention on their work, not pretty girls. Distraction can be dangerous when you're handling molten glass."

"It's wonderful to watch though." Sarah was gazing around, wide-eyed and openmouthed. "I had no idea that's how you make windows. No wonder they're so expensive."

"And now that you've mentioned windows," Father said,

"you didn't need to come in here to ask me for more."

"I know. That is—" Meg took a deep breath. "I didn't come in here to ask for more windows. I mean, yes, I would like them and would like to make whoever smashed the other ones pay for them. But I have to tell you something else."

Father and Sarah both stared at her, faces puzzled. Father raised one hand to gesture for someone behind Meg to wait. Meg forced herself not to look.

"Go ahead," Father said.

Meg gulped. "Father, you can tell Mr. Grassick he needn't make so many glasses. Not because—because I don't want them." She spoke the last words in a rush. "I do. They're the most beautiful glasses I've ever seen. But I know they take a long time to make and that I planned not to announce the betrothal until they were done. But if he doesn't make so many, maybe he can make new windows instead." Out of breath she sagged in her chair, as though she had just set down a heavy burden.

Behind her, someone cleared his throat. In front of her, Sarah's face had gone blank, and Father frowned, but not as though he were angry. He looked—sad.

When no one spoke, Meg added, "So I had to come here straightaway to prevent any unnecessary work."

"I appreciate your honesty, daughter." Father stepped away from the desk. "Will you excuse me a moment?"

"Of course." Meg gathered her cloak around her, felt something sharp prick her hand, and remembered the kitten in her pocket. "Would you like us to leave now?"

"No, no, I'd rather you stay for a few minutes." Father walked around Meg. "Thank you for finishing that bowl, Grassick. I believe Mrs. Beckett will be pleased with it. Let's take it out back for packing."

Their footfalls rang on the stone floor then died amid the hiss of fires and tinkle of glass falling onto hard surfaces.

"You really don't want to marry Joseph badly, do you?" Sarah whispered.

"You know I don't."

Sarah shook her head. "But I didn't know you would go to such lengths to avoid it."

"I went too far, and now I've been punished by maybe not being able to have my school open after all."

"Punished by whom? I mean, who knows what your plan was?"

"No one except the Lord."

"God doesn't work that way." Sarah drew her nearly straight brows together. "At least I don't think He does."

"I'm supposed to marry Joseph because it's what my father wants for me, and I'm trying to avoid it. So why should I get what I want?"

"Because you thought the Lord wanted you to open the school for the sake of other children?" Sarah suggested.

Meg didn't have a chance to respond. Father returned at that moment with Colin and Joseph accompanying him. Colin met Meg's glance for a heartbeat, gave her a half smile, then spun on his heel and paced to the back of the factory. Father and Joseph approached the desk.

"Good day, ladies." Joseph bowed.

Sunlight drew out the gold in his hair, spinning it around his head like a halo. He was indeed handsome, probably better looking than Colin.

"Isaac"—Joseph nodded to Father—"has asked me if I'll accompany you ladies home."

And he was nice. She should really want to spend her life with such a good man.

"Thank you." Meg rose, cupping the now squirming kitten in her hand. "Father?" She gave him a questioning glance.

He returned it with a gentle smile. "Grassick has offered to work extra hours to make the windows for your school and to finish the goblets."

"He—but—" Meg swallowed a sudden lump in her throat.

"We'll talk this evening." Father shook Joseph's hand. "Thank you and hurry right back. I want to show you the new windows made with the flint glass. So much clearer, if a bit expensive to produce."

"Maybe not if there's less waste and less need for framing." Joseph laughed. "But we won't bore the ladies with this talk of business matters."

Meg wasn't bored. On the contrary, she was intrigued. She didn't think she should be asking to know more at that moment. She'd received a reprieve.

With a bob of a curtsy to Father, she led the way outside. What had been a pleasant autumn day earlier felt chilly after the heat of the glassworks. She gathered her cloak around her. At the movement her pocket meowed.

"Do you always carry cats in your pocket?" Joseph asked.

Sarah laughed. "You know our Meg. She's always rescuing something."

"Indeed. It's one of the lovable things about her." Joseph held out an arm for each lady. "I'm so pleased she's going to rescue me from a lonely life. And rescue my house from neglect."

"Does Peter feel like you're rescuing him?" Meg asked, blushing over the praise while, she had to admit to herself, pleased by it.

"More like he's rescuing me." Sarah's husky chuckle mingled with the rising wind in the trees. "I won't have to share the kitchen with my mother when I've a mind to bake."

"Meg won't ever have to set foot in the kitchen." To Meg, Joseph's shoulders seemed to straighten and his chin rose a notch as he made this declaration.

She frowned over his pride.

"I have a cook, as well as a housekeeper," he announced.

"But I like to bake," she protested. "My sugar buns are even better than Ilse's, and she taught me to make them."

The instant the words were out of her mouth, she wished she'd bitten her tongue instead of speaking them. She was criticizing Joseph for being boastful—then boasting herself.

"At least she says they are," Meg murmured.

"They are." Sarah toed a pinecone out of her path. "You'll be denying yourself a treat if you don't let her bake now and again, Joseph."

"Well, of course if she wants to." Joseph pressed Meg's hand against his side for a moment too long. "I know how Margaret likes to have her own way."

"I want to be obedient," Meg said then added, "to God."

Sarah gave out an unladylike snort she hastily covered with a cough.

Fortunately they reached the lane to the Jordan farm at that moment, and Meg looked to the west, where the sun was beginning to drop into the horizon.

"You should take Sarah straight home. If you walk me up to the house, it'll be dark before you get back to the glassworks, and you don't have a lantern."

"Wise you are." Joseph took her hand from his arm and raised it to his lips. "Good evening, my dear."

From beyond his bent head, Meg met Sarah's eyes and read a surprise she hoped wasn't reflected on her own face. She'd never had her hand kissed before. Other than by her parents, she'd never been kissed before.

She didn't think she liked it.

With an effort she managed not to snatch her fingers free and said something pleasant to Sarah like seeing her at church. Necessary pleasantries over, Meg spun on the flat heel of her slipper and strode up the lane with more haste than dignity or grace.

"I should like him," she made herself say aloud. "He cares for me. I should like him. He cares for me. I should. . ."

No amount of repetition made the words come true. She should or should not do a lot of things she did or did not do. Even Saint Paul had suffered from this affliction. Yet he had been obedient to God even when He made him do things that would send him to prison.

"I will marry him." As she entered the front door of the house, she changed it to a declaration. "I will. I will. I—oops."

She'd forgotten the cat was in her pocket.

She took him out to the stable to join his siblings and friends. They were feasting on some scraps of meat from the supper preparations. His tiny nose twitched, and he scrambled out of Meg's hand and raced across the yard to push his way into the food.

In her bedchamber she washed her face and wrapped a fresh fichu around her neck, one of white linen with a lace edging. Her eyes remained a bit puffy, but her cheeks no longer bore the marks of her tears. Once she had brushed her hair and replaced a few pins, she was ready to help Ilse with the last of the supper preparations. She wasn't sure she would ever be ready to meet her father for the talk he said they would have later.

Yet he hadn't seemed angry. Shocked, distressed, yes, but not angry. Then again, he might have been exhibiting self-control if Joseph and Colin Grassick were within earshot.

When she heard the front door open, her heart began to throb in her chest like galloping hooves. Hastily she picked up the pitcher of lemonade that had been cooling in the springhouse and carried it into the dining room to fill the glasses.

Father entered the room in minutes. Shadows made his eyes appear deep set and dark, and two lines cut grooves on either side of his mouth. But he gave Meg a smile and pulled out her chair.

"You look like your mother tonight," he told her. "She was fond of wearing a white collar with lace."

Meg glowed at his compliment. "Thank you."

"So what do we have for supper tonight?"

"Ragout with noodles."

"Ah, one of my favorite dishes of Ilse's."

They ate in near silence. Despite his claim of the meal being one of his favorites, he ate less than usual, barely managing to finish the plateful Meg served him. Seeing his lack of appetite, Meg lost what was left of hers and sent Ilse back to the kitchen, muttering about wastefulness.

"Take it to the single workers," Meg suggested, following her with the dirty dishes.

"Ach, you know we only have one of those now that Thaddeus has married. It's to that Scot this'll go, and deserving he is, working so hard and eating bachelor fare."

She carried the coffeepot back into the dining room. "Shall I join you, Father?"

"Yes, I have a few things to discuss with you." He folded his hands on the still-pristine tablecloth.

Meg poured coffee for each of them, though she didn't want it, and waited for him to speak.

He cleared his throat. "Why don't you want to marry Joseph?"

"It's too silly." She pressed her hands against her warm cheeks. "It makes sense to me, but when I say it out loud, it sounds—childish."

"To me, Margaret, you are a child."

"I'm not, though. I'm an old maid nearly. You've said so yourself."

"Yes, well, just try to say it."

"I'd like to say it's only because I don't love him, which is true, but I know you and Momma didn't love one another either and grew to over time."

"Marriages were arranged more often in those days than they are now."

Then why had he arranged hers?

Meg tamped down the spirit of rebellion.

"Go on." Father's face showed no expression. "If it's not only that you don't love him, what else is it?"

"He's not my choice." Meg blurted out the words before she lost her courage.

Father said nothing for several minutes, long minutes in which a log fell in the fireplace, sending a shower of sparks spiraling up the chimney and making her jump. Tedious minutes in which she had to clasp her hands together tightly enough to make her knuckles white to prevent herself from drumming her nails on the table.

"And what sort of man would you choose?" Father asked abruptly.

"I don't know." An image of emerald green eyes flashed through her mind, and she amended, "Joseph seems unfriendly."

Except for that kiss on her hand. That was too friendly.

Although she had spoken little to Colin Grassick, Meg felt closer to him after those conversations than she did to Joseph, whom she'd known all her life. Colin spoke of things in his heart. Joseph spoke of—things. Things like his big house. Things like having a cook and a housekeeper.

"He cares too much about his possessions." She spoke on a wave of inspiration.

"Ah." Father gave her his half smile. "But all those possessions will allow you to carry on your charitable work. You can start a whole farm for wayward cats. And provide every child in the county with chapter books."

"If he lets me," she muttered.

"Hmm. Well, yes." Father drummed his fingers on the table. He gazed toward the curtained windows for another minute then he turned to Meg and covered one of her hands with his. "I can't go back on my word to Joseph about your marrying him. I made a promise to your mother, too, but I broke it. And now—Joseph has agreed to postpone the announcement of the wedding until after the New Year."

Meg's eyes stung. Father had broken a promise to Momma? It seemed unbelievable.

"And the wedding?"

"That's still in the spring. The twenty-eighth day of April." Father's lips flattened. "Don't ask me to postpone that, too. Please, for my sake, this wedding must take place."

seven

The vacant windows of the schoolhouse seemed to glower at Colin as he passed, accusing him of shirking his promise to replace the glass. Given the opportunity, he would be back at the glasshouse working on the panes. But this Saturday afternoon Mr. Jordan insisted he take time off. The great furnaces needed to cool so the pits beneath the fire grates could be cleaned of ashes. So Colin took Thad's offer of the use of his fishing equipment and headed for a pool in the creek the junior glassblower recommended was a fine place.

"You catch them and my wife will cook them," Thad offered.

The pool lay just beyond the school, and Colin couldn't stop himself from hoping Miss Jordan would find a reason to visit her building or go for a walk with her friend Sarah Thompson or call on any number of people along the road in his direction, including the church. She probably wouldn't see him tucked amid the dense growth of trees along the water, but he would hear her coming. He found himself turning to peer through the branches every time he caught the sound of a foot scraping on the hard-packed earth of the lane. Fortunately for the sake of his line and pole, few people traversed the stretch of road in the middle of the afternoon, even on a Saturday. Too few, since none proved to be Meg Jordan with her light, quick tread and bouncing curls.

Twice Colin found himself starting to pray she would come along, but he stopped before fully forming the words. He should be praying to forget about her. No one had told him not to speak to her, even after Mr. Jordan had been displeased to find them chatting in his kitchen and ordered Colin back to the glassworks. But Colin knew wanting to be near her was wrong. He must think about his work, about his family, about earning a future for them that would make up for what he had caused them to lose.

Yet every time he saw her, his heart lifted. A glance, a smile, a nod from her made him forget the emptiness he had made of his life. To Meg Jordan, who he was and what he'd done didn't seem to matter. He told her the truth about his father, and she still looked at him as though—

She looked at him as though she liked him, and that was wrong. She was marrying another man. Even if the announcement of the betrothal hadn't been made official yet, Colin reminded himself of the truth with each amethyst goblet he produced.

He also knew another truth: Meg Jordan didn't want to marry Joseph Pyle. Since her father obviously loved her, Colin couldn't work out why the man was so insistent that she wed Mr. Pyle. Pure greed? The Pyle fortune was well known in the county, Colin had learned in his four weeks in America. Yet Jordan was a kind and generous man. Marrying off his daughter to a man she didn't care for simply out of a desire to have her marry wealth didn't seem to fit the situation.

A tug on his line stopped Colin from pursuing that thread of consideration further. With pulling on the fish's part, and persistence on his, and enough splashing to mimic a flailing swimmer, Colin landed a fish with a greenish back and silvery sides. He didn't recognize it and wasn't certain it was edible but decided to keep it. Catch in hand, he turned to place it in the basket he'd brought for the purpose and discovered his bucket of bait had disappeared.

Movement through the trees and a muffled giggle hinted at the cause of the disappearance. Throwing the fish into the creel, he shoved through the foliage in time to see five boys charging toward the road. A bucket banged against the leg of the smallest of them. All held their hands to their mouths.

Chuckling, Colin lunged after them. "Halt right there, lads," he called to them.

To his surprise they stopped and faced him. He kept going. In another two yards he intended to stop and lecture them on stealing. He wanted to be close to them, close enough to look down at even the tallest of them.

One boy moved, scooping something from the bucket. Long, brown objects sailed toward Colin. He ducked to avoid an onslaught of worms, and someone behind him screamed.

Colin straightened and turned in time to see Meg Jordan pluck a worm from the shoulder of her cloak and throw it back at the boys.

"How did you miss something the size of Mr. Grassick, children?" She was laughing. Her eyes sparkled.

Colin thought the sun had come out and the temperature had risen to summertime. Tongue-tied, he glanced from her to the boys, who seemed equally struck mute.

"Whose worms are those?" she asked, tilting her head to one side so a curl bobbed against her cheek.

Colin clenched his fingers against a wish to tuck the errant strand behind her ear.

The boys ducked their heads and scuffed their clogs in the dirt.

"I was doing a wee bit of fishing," Colin managed. "While I was bringing in my catch, these lads decided to have a bit of fun with me."

"First cats, now worms." She clucked her tongue. "I don't think they should get away with it. What shall we make them do, Mr. Grassick?"

"We was just playin'," the youngest one cried. "We would have brought 'em back."

"But you all threw them at him and struck me." She shook her head. A limp worm dangled from the brim of her felt hat like a broken plume. "Mr. Grassick, what do you think?"

"I think they'll need to be in the front row of the school when it opens," Colin said.

Meg looked delighted. Expressions of horror crossed the boys' faces.

"An excellent notion." Meg nodded. "The first Monday in January, boys. Be there, or I'll send Mr. Grassick to collect you. Now run along, and don't go stealing things or harming living creatures."

"And I'll take that bucket back." Colin collected the bucket as the youngest one dropped it and fled.

"They don't have a mother, I learned," Meg said. "And their father is busy all the time with the charcoal burner. If I can make them come to school, it will give them something to do an hour or two a day and maybe keep them out of trouble."

"Aye, they're not bad bairns. They simply need a bit of supervision." Pail in one hand, Colin stepped close enough to her to pluck the worm from her hat. "The color does not suit you."

She made a face, laughed, then lifted her chin and looked directly into his eyes. "Thank you."

"Aye. That is, you're welcome." He swallowed. "You're not squeamish about the creepy crawly things then?"

"No, I grew up fishing with my father in these waters before he decided to reopen the glassworks and got too busy." She smiled. "I don't clean them though. E–ew."

"I only have the one pole, but I'm willing to share." He clasped both hands on the handle of the bucket. "If you think 'twould be all right to join me."

"It's all right. I'm on my way back from the church. I was trying to see if they have any extra benches I can use for the school. They don't, so now I'm not promised to anyone." She sighed and muttered, "Yet."

That word *yet* reminded Colin to merely enjoy her company and think no more of it than a pleasant time with a pretty lass. If he told himself that enough, he might believe it. For the moment he couldn't stop his heart from leaping like a salmon.

"Then, by all means, join me, madam." He offered her his arm.

She took it, and they returned to the pool.

"Who told you about this place?" she asked. "Or did you find it on your own?"

"Thad told me." He retrieved his pole, untangled the line, and hooked a worm. "You may have the first cast. Do you need any help?"

"I should go all missish and say yes." She took the pole and sent the baited hook arcing into the water with scarcely a ripple. "But I'd be fibbing."

"Apparently so." He stooped to gather wet grasses to keep his catch cool and damp, though the misty day would do much of that. Beside him Meg stood motionless except for occasionally moving the tip of the pole.

"You're very good at this." He straightened and gazed down on the crown of her hat, over which curled a pink feather. "How old were you when you last fished?"

"A clever way of asking my age, since you know the glassworks have been open for five years." She leaned a little forward. "I was sixteen."

"I had no intention of being that calculating. My apologies for being so bold."

"None necessary. Hmm." She gave her line a little tug. "Everyone in the county knows I'm practically on the shelf. Finicky Meg—ah yes, I have a bite."

With calm and skill she reeled in the fish, took one look at the whiskered orange beast, and made a noise of disgust.

"Catfish." She shuddered. "Not something to my liking, but go ahead and keep it. Some people love them."

"Aye, I'll take them all to Martha Dalbow. She can feed

them to her pig if she doesn't want them."

"And save the inner bits for your cat." She handed him the pole, allowing him to remove the fish from the hook and rebait it. "How is the wee beastie?"

The sound of the Scots expression on her lips sent his insides quivering. "Fat and spoiled." He cast. "How is your wanderer?"

"Still up to his tricks. I expect I'll be teaching my class one day, and he'll be yowling in the tree outside the windows."

"Some creatures don't have enough sense to stay home where they're loved and safe." He fixed his gaze on the pond.

It lay as still as a mirror, reflecting trees, the gray sky, and their figures side by side on the bank, quiet, comfortable, companionable. It was a vision he would happily keep in his head. In his heart.

"How did the son of a Highland fisherman become a Lowland glassblower?"

Her question yanked him back to the way things really were—him in no position to think about her as anything more than his master's daughter.

"I found a piece of glass on the shore one day." He focused on the past, his father's face as he told him he didn't want to go to sea day after day. "Somehow it managed not to break on the rocks. Probably washed up from a ship. I do not ken. It was only a bowl, but the color was a clear amber like your eyes." He kept his gaze away from her face so he could not see her reaction to his offhand compliment. "The curve of the bowl was so fine I wanted to ken how 'twas done. I asked the minister, he being a learned man from Edinburgh. He told me about the glassblowers, and I had to see for myself. So I sold the bowl to a *sassenach*—an Englishman—visiting the Highlands for the grouse hunting, and I left."

"Did you know you were an artist before then?" Her voice was soft, as though she didn't want the birds in the treetops to hear her.

He snorted. "I am nay artist, Miss Jordan. I am a craftsman."

"You're an artist." Her reflection told him she'd tilted her face toward him. "I know the difference between the two."

"Ah well. Perhaps I have a bit of a gift." He ducked his head, warm with pleasure at her compliment. "I did a bit of drawing with sticks in the dirt, but we didn't have the silver for paper and pencils."

"Do you think your father truly begrudged your seeking a profession that better suited your skills and God-given gifts?"

"Nay, he was not that sort. But I could have sent the money home to help with the bairns. I was a selfish youth who cost them all too much."

"Oh Colin." She laid her hand on his arm.

In the same instant, the tip of his pole swooped toward the water. His foot slid on the grassy bank. With a weight on the hook and thrown off balance, Colin toppled toward the pond.

"Let go," Meg cried.

Contrary to her words, she caught hold—of him. Her arms encircled his waist and, slight as it was, her weight helped him regain his balance and find solid footing.

Colin landed another fish he didn't recognize, something bluish and full of fight, but far enough up on the bank he risked setting down the pole without worrying the catch would flop back into the water and pull Thad's equipment after it.

"I couldn't let go of Thad's fishing pole," Colin said in an even tone. "He may not have another."

"No—no, you couldn't." Meg released him and moved away, out of his sight, away from a reflection in the pool.

Colin faced her. She held her hand to her lips, and she squeezed her eyes shut.

"Lass, what's the trouble?" He raised one hand but stopped short of touching her.

She shook her head, and an odd choking noise came from her throat.

"Lass, are you—" He narrowed his eyes. "Are you laughing at me?"

She nodded, and the mirth burst from her. "I am so sorry." She took a shuddering breath. "But you admit we looked a bit silly."

"Aye, well, I never was verra good at the dancing."

They laughed. They fished together; they talked of growing up in places far different from each other yet sharing a common thread of learning of a faith in God.

"I abandoned mine in the city," Colin admitted. "But I turned my heart back to the Lord after my father died."

"Then good came of it." Meg frowned at the darkening sky. "I fail in my willfulness. I just want things the way I want them."

Colin smiled into her eyes, knowing they must go soon, knowing this was an interlude they would likely never share again. "Aye, I ken what you mean. I wish things were different."

"They will be." Meg clasped her hands in front of her. "If ever I wanted things to be the way I want them, it's more afternoons like this—for us."

eight

If only she knew why her father insisted she marry Joseph, Meg thought she could persuade him not to go through with the wedding plans. Father said he wanted her to marry because she needed to be settled with a home of her own. Yet now he told her she mustn't call off the inevitable announcement of the betrothal for his sake. For her sake, she must learn what was wrong.

If she could hold off the wedding announcement that long.

Briefly she considered telling Joseph outright that she found her interests lay elsewhere. The risk to Colin stopped her. So she prayed for things to change and worked harder to get her school ready to start the first Monday of the New Year.

Seating was still a problem she hadn't solved. The minister promised to give her some slates and chalk someone had donated to the church, but other than that, he couldn't help her with furnishings. And the windows were still missing glass.

"It seems like it won't open after all," she told Sarah one afternoon.

Sarah's mother was pinning up the hem of a merino traveling dress in which Sarah would accompany her new husband for a week in New York, meeting his family. The deep green complemented Sarah's rich red brown hair and drew out the color in her cheeks.

"You're so beautiful." Meg poured enthusiasm into her friend's new wardrobe and set worries about her own marriage and school aside. "Peter will fall even more in love with you than he already is."

Sarah laughed and blushed. Her hazel eyes grew dreamy.

With the wedding less than three weeks away, she thought of little else than her husband-to-be and her home. Meg rejoiced for her friend, while feeling a twinge of loneliness cutting inside her. Sarah would never have the same freedom to run about with Meg as she enjoyed now. Yet Sarah wanted the change because she'd met the man she loved and wanted to spend her life with.

Later, when Peter arrived for dinner, Meg watched him and Sarah exchange glances and knew she had spoken the complete truth when she told Sarah she couldn't wed a man until she found one who looked at her that way. Joseph didn't gaze at her with love. She hadn't yet put a name to the emotion in his glances, but it wasn't devotion.

Quiet, she accepted Peter's offer to walk her home rather than Sarah's invitation to spend the night. Father was leaving for Philadelphia the following day, and she wanted to ensure his bags were packed to his satisfaction.

"I'll return tomorrow." Meg kissed Sarah's cheek and headed out for the short walk down the road to home.

Once out of earshot of the house, Peter brought up the subject of glass. "It's a little late, I know, but I thought I could order some fine pieces for our new house. I was thinking candlesticks or glass globes for the wall sconces. Maybe for Christmas?"

"I don't know, but come by the glassworks early in the morning if you can and discuss it with Father before he leaves for the city." She smiled as a thought struck her. "I could go with you to help pick out some ideas."

"I'd like that." Peter heaved a sigh of relief. "I want everything perfect for Sarah."

"She doesn't need perfection, Peter." Meg smiled up at the young man she'd known for many years. He was tall and slim, and his dark hair and eyes were an attractive contrast to Sarah's vivid coloring.

"She would like a kitten, too," Meg added.

Peter laughed. "I'd rather give her glass baubles, but if she wants a cat, she can have one."

"Good. She can pick one out when you return from New York. I found three more abandoned near my school, so that makes nine I've rescued in the past month."

They reached the Jordans' house. Peter bade her good night with the promise to see her in the morning then strode off down the drive, whistling.

Meg fairly skipped to the door.

&

With the prospect of even catching a glimpse of Colin the next day, she was too excited to sleep well or eat much breakfast.

"You're not sickening, are you?" Ilse asked.

"No, just excited."

"Ah, the friend's wedding." Ilse nodded and carried the oatmeal porridge away.

"I'm going over to the glassworks to help Mr. Strawn pick out a gift for Sarah."

"And that's put you off your food?" Ilse gave her a narrow-eyed look.

"I'd better finish packing." Meg bolted up the steps to her bedchamber.

For the week Father would be in Philadelphia to conduct business, something to do with the glassworks, Meg would stay with Sarah's family. They were happy to have her help with the wedding so close. Too close. Signaling the nearness of Christmas and then the first of the year and the end of her own freedom.

It also meant the opening of her school. She must think about that. Her school and a room full of children needing to learn.

She concentrated on packing until Peter, as he promised, arrived to walk over to the glassworks. The air was clear but cold, and frost still clung to the grass. It kept their steps brisk, and they reached the factory before they had time to exchange more than pleasantries.

Father stood just outside the door, speaking with Joseph. Meg's heart plummeted, her excitement over the possibility of seeing Colin for a moment or two evaporating like the frost beneath the sun's feeble rays. Nonetheless, she managed a polite greeting and explained the purpose of the visit.

"I really need to be on my way." Father looked regretful. "We can't keep the horses waiting in this cold, and they'll be harnessed up by now."

Even as he spoke, the rumble of carriage wheels and hooves resounded from the road.

"They're here now," Father added.

"But it's a fine sale." Joseph laughed. "Sales are money, Jordan. And we all need to make money."

The corners of Father's mouth tightened, but he softened them to smile at Meg. "The designs are on a shelf behind my desk, Margaret. Why don't you take Peter in and show him. Call Grassick or Dalbow for assistance if you need any." He hesitated then added, "And fetch Mrs. Dalbow, so there's another female with you."

"I'll do that." Meg kissed his cheek. "Have a good journey, Father."

She walked off with an even, dignified stride until she was out of sight, then she dashed through the yard, past the outbuildings and along the walkway to the Dalbow cottage.

Martha Dalbow was a petite, pretty young woman Meg had known all her life. Her father had been a laborer on the Pyle farm, and Meg and Martha played together as children until Meg went to school in Burgen County in the northern part of the state. Now they exchanged smiles and waves at church, but Martha married a glassblower and wasn't invited to the same houses as Meg.

Greeting her childhood friend, Meg experienced a spurt

of rebellion and decided to be friendlier with Martha in the future, especially now that Sarah would live farther away.

"So you're going to get married, too." Martha trotted alongside Meg on their way back to the glassworks, her golden curls bobbing with every bouncy step. "I always thought you'd be first."

"It's not certain." Meg figured if she said it enough it would be so. "I haven't said yes."

"Then I'll save my congratulations."

They reached the group of men standing near the door. Father had gone, and Peter and Joseph were engaged in a discussion about the price of shipping goods out of the country. Peter broke off as soon as Meg and Martha arrived, but Joseph took several minutes to finish expounding on tariffs before acknowledging Meg's arrival. He said nothing to Martha. He offered Meg his arm, leaving Martha to follow.

Meg declined the offer and preceded him inside, her hand on Martha's elbow to bring her along.

The heat enveloped her like an extra cloak. Although the desk lay to her left, her gaze shot to the right almost of its own volition, seeking, finding, resting on Colin in his corner. He was working with a piece of glass the consistency of thickened caramel, applying tongs and a cutter to stretch and twist the hot, shimmering mass. Meg's heart suddenly felt the same as that hot glass—malleable, twisted, compressed. She heard voices around her but couldn't comprehend what they said.

"Margaret." Joseph's tone sharpened, and he grasped her arm.

She started. "I—I'm sorry." She swung toward Father's desk. "I'm fascinated by the process of making glass."

And the man making it.

Martha nodded and smiled but said nothing until they all tried to make sense of the diagrams drawn on wide sheets of paper.

"I'll fetch one of the men," she whispered, then she darted off.

Meg watched Martha's progress through the factory, around the furnaces, and past the benches of the blowers. She paused by her husband, who shook his head, then she walked around him and out of sight. Meg tensed, waiting for Martha to reappear, waiting for Colin to appear. Waiting, anticipating, hoping—

"Margaret." Joseph's sharp tone returned Meg to the men beside her.

She blinked up at him. "Did you say something to me?"

Joseph and Peter gave her questioning glances.

"I was woolgathering." Meg turned her back on the workroom. "Peter, I think this design is a glass globe for a wall sconce. See the crimped edges at the top?" She traced a wavy line along the upper edge of a design. "Of course, it's a little too round, so—maybe. . ." Her voice trailed off.

She hadn't heard his footfalls above the clang and clatter of equipment and roar of the furnaces, but she sensed him, caught the scent of smoke and the tang of the silica.

"'Tis a vase." Colin's hand joined hers on the sketch. "See how the bottom is rounded? A sconce would be straight to fit into the holder."

"How silly of me." She felt breathless, too warm in her heavy cloak and wool dress. "I don't think Peter—Mr. Strawn—wants vases, do you, Peter? You mentioned sconces or maybe glasses. Glasses would take longer, since you'd need several, so maybe—" She snapped her teeth together.

She was talking too much.

"Let Grassick help Peter." Joseph's voice was as cold and brittle and sharp as an icicle. "I will walk you home."

"No." Meg stepped away from the desk, away from Colin, and away from Joseph. "I'll go to Martha's house until Peter is ready to help carry my things to Sarah's."

"If you like." Joseph's eyes gleamed pale blue. "I'll see you at church on Sunday." He stalked to the front door of the glassworks.

Meg caught sight of Martha talking to her husband again

and waved her over.

They exited out the back door. As Meg turned to pull the heavy panel closed behind her, she caught Colin's eyes upon her and smiled, and her stomach fluttered.

She closed her eyes for a moment to gain her composure, and when she opened them again, Colin stood with his back to her. Her belly settled, and she trotted off behind Martha, an apology on her lips.

"I don't need to stay, since you probably have work to do, Martha. I can walk home on my own."

"But I'd like you to stay." Martha lowered her eyes. "I'm learning how to knit and would love to show someone what I'm making Thad."

"And I'd love to see it."

More time than Meg anticipated passed with Martha. She found herself settling into the cozy kitchen with its herbs hanging from the ceiling and heavy pot simmering over the fire, sending the wonderful aroma of venison throughout the cottage. The entire home seemed to embrace Meg with its plain but comfortable furnishings and embroidered samplers of Bible verses decorating the whitewashed walls. Martha showed Meg everything, her face glowing.

"Will you teach me to knit?" Meg asked. "It's so useful."

"But it's not very ladylike, is it?"

"Neither is fishing, but I do that, too."

Martha laughed. "I heard." She tilted her head and glanced at Meg from the corner of one blue eye. "Colin is a wonderful man."

"Yes." Meg fingered the scarf Martha was knitting, admiring the smoothness of the stitches. "And talented."

"And works for your father."

"It doesn't matter."

But Meg knew it did. It mattered to her father. It mattered to Colin. It should matter to her.

"I'd better be on my way." She stood abruptly. "I want to visit you again. You can teach me to knit, and if I get any girls in my school, I can teach them. Where do I find the needles and yarn?"

Information in hand, Meg returned to the glassworks. Peter seemed to be occupying his time watching the work at hand. Meg wanted to stay but knew she shouldn't. If she were wise, she would leave the glassworks and not return.

She didn't think she was wise—only prudent enough to not mention Colin's name to Peter, to Sarah, to God in her prayers. She tried not to think about him. Like not thinking about her upcoming betrothal, she hoped a lack of thought would make it go away, whatever it was, the tightening inside her whenever she saw him. It was a feeling like she would burst into tears if she couldn't see him and song when she did.

Except she didn't see him. With Father gone, she couldn't even contrive an excuse for visiting the glassworks. Staying with the Thompsons, she couldn't get over to the Dalbow cottage and perhaps encounter him there unless she came up with a good excuse.

The idea came to her while she and Sarah unpacked linens in Sarah's new home. The stacks of sheets, pillowcases, and towels had been stored in wooden crates lined with muslin and sprinkled with lavender, as Sarah had finished embroidering her and Peter's initials on them. Fatigued from a restless night, Meg sat on an unopened crate and suddenly knew how to solve her problem of seating for the students she hoped to have at her school.

"Packing crates!" She leaped to her feet. "We'll use packing crates for benches."

"That's a good idea." Sarah tucked an armful of sheets in the linen press. "You're welcome to take these, but it won't be enough."

"I hope it won't be enough. But Father has acres of them at the glassworks. I'm sure he won't care if I take a few for seats. Shall we go see?"

"Now?" Sarah shook her head. "Your father isn't home or there."

"No one will be there. It's Saturday afternoon, and they stop work early to let the furnaces cool for cleaning."

Not waiting for Sarah to agree, Meg ran down the steps to the entryway and snatched her cloak off a stand by the door. "I'll just run up and look at what's available and see if they're the right size."

"No, don't go alone. The walk will be good." Sarah started down the steps. "If I breathe any more lavender, I'll get a headache."

Cloaks tucked around them against the bite of the early December wind, they strolled along the road. Wood smoke from cooking fires scented the air, and a handful of snowflakes danced around them.

"If it snows," Meg grumbled, "everything in the school will get wet without the windows."

"It won't snow yet. There's sunshine over there." Sarah gestured to the west.

Sunlight glowed around the edges of the clouds like a promise. Meg hugged herself and increased her pace. Sometimes Colin worked extra hours. Maybe today. . .

Although a curl of smoke drifted lazily into the brightening sky from one of the two chimneys at the glassworks, the building was empty, the fires banked in the furnaces.

"They must have just left." Meg closed the door then paused, frowning at it. "But I can't believe they left without locking it."

"Maybe they'll be right back." Sarah tugged on Meg's arm. "We shouldn't be inside without anyone here."

"No, but it's awfully messy. They usually clean up at the end of the day." Though not liking the glassworks left open and unkempt, Meg allowed Sarah to lead her around the building to the shed where packing crates rose in stacks higher than their heads.

"I think these will work." Sarah used her hands to

measure one crate. "They're high enough for children."

"And they're sturdy, since they have to hold glass. Oh, here's someone." Meg glanced over her shoulder, hoping, then suppressing a sigh of disappointment.

Thaddeus Dalbow, not Colin, strode into the yard. "Miss Meg, Miss Sarah, may I be of assistance?"

"I want to look at packing crates." Meg glanced toward the factory building. "Are you the one working late today?" She tried to sound casual. "I thought it was only Mr. Grassick who worked extra hours."

Sarah's breath hissed through her teeth, and Meg realized she'd given herself away just saying his name.

"It is." Thad shoved a lock of unruly hair away from his face. "But there was an accident."

nine

Colin knew he should be at church and not working, however charitable the work. He heard his mother's admonitions about the need for worship and teaching ringing with nearly every breath he took. But at church he saw Meg, and seeing Meg had begun to hurt as much as did his left hand.

"You understand, do You not, Lord?" As he often did, he prayed while he worked alone.

Today's project took him to Meg's school, a building that appeared to have been an old cottage no one used any longer. Instead of Mr. Jordan having to hire a carpenter to fit the new glass panes into the wooden frames, Colin had offered to do the work. With the glass finished, he decided to risk someone disapproving of him working on a Sunday and set the windows back into the school for Meg's next visit.

"When else would I be having the daylight?" Colin thought something must be wrong if he was trying to justify his actions to the Lord. If he needed to justify them, they couldn't be right.

That knowledge didn't stop him from lifting the first pane of glass from its nest of straw and sliding it into the frame. Around him a few birds chirped and the air smelled clean. He caught a hint of water with the wind blowing from the direction of the nearby bay, and his heart ached with the wish to see his family. He had abandoned them fifteen years ago with scarcely a backward glance, yet now that his father's death had brought them together again, he didn't want to be apart from them.

"So you should stop thinking of the master's daughter, my lad."

Think of Meg he did—too often. He'd ruined a perfectly good candlestick when she walked into the glassworks on Wednesday morning, as bright and effervescent as the morning itself. The excuse to go near her came as a gift, a blessing, and he exerted every bit of willpower he possessed not to run through the factory to her side.

And Joseph Pyle, that man to whom she would be wed too soon, stood near her, too, glaring at Colin as though he intended to shrivel him like last year's apples.

"She can never be yours, lad," Colin cautioned himself over the first pane of glass.

He had no business even considering more than a polite exchange of words with her for however long he remained in Salem County. She was his master's daughter, and he had a family who needed him more than Meg Jordan needed anything.

"Keep your mind on your work and the Lord," he admonished himself.

As though to prove he wasn't doing enough of the latter, church bells began to ring across the countryside, pure and melodic. Soon worshippers would travel along the road, returning to their homes or visiting with friends and neighbors. She would pass by, too. He wanted her to see him and stop. He knew she shouldn't.

His hand throbbed, and he paused to soak it in a bucket of cold water, as Ilse Weber had told him he should. She was right. It wasn't the first time he'd burned himself while learning to manipulate hot glass. But this was the first time the burn hadn't been his fault. Not that he could prove that or do more than speculate how the accident occurred.

The water diminishing the ache in his hand, he resumed his work with the window, fitting a pane into the frame and holding it with the uninjured half of his left hand, so he could apply the caulking with his right. The position proved awkward, and when he heard her voice, the glass slipped out of his hold.

He caught it an instant before it struck the ground and broke. The sharp edge nicked his palm. He frowned, figuring it was what he deserved for not resting and worshipping on a Sunday.

And for thinking of Meg Jordan instead of the Lord.

"Mother would be ashamed of you, lad," he muttered.

"I should think she would be indeed." Meg's voice brimmed with laughter. "You should have been in church or home resting that hand."

"Ah, you sound like a schoolmistress." He laughed, too, and turned to face her, his left hand outstretched. "I could not tie a proper cravat for attending the kirk, and I'm hoping the Lord will forgive my work if 'tis for a good cause and not personal gain."

"Oh Colin." She cradled his hand in both of hers, the silk of her gloves snagging on his rough skin. "I was distressed when Thad told us about your accident." She touched the blisters on his palm and pinkie finger so gently she gave him no pain. "How did it happen?"

"'Tis what I'd like to ken myself." He frowned at his hand.

Her gaze flashed to his face. "What do you mean?"

"I mean my grate—you ken where the pipe rests?—'twas hot enough to burn when it should have been as cool as this glass."

"Colin." She curled her fingers around the uninjured part of his hand. "How? I mean, were you in the glassworks alone?"

"I thought I was, but someone could have sneaked in while I was mixing the silica."

"Why? Why would anyone want to hurt you?"

"'Tis not unheard of in the glasshouses. Envy. Fear for their positions. Malice." He set down the pane of glass he still held and smoothed the crease between her brows with the tip of his finger. "Do not fash yourself, lass. I'll be more careful in the future."

"I'll tell my father—"

"Nay, do not. 'Twill cause unnecessary trouble. I'll heal."

"But, Colin—"

"Go now." He extracted his grip from hers. "You shouldn't be here, you ken. You're an engaged lady, and he's likely wondering where you are."

"We're not engaged yet." She grimaced. "Father still wants me to marry Mr. Pyle, but nothing is official until after the first of the year. And I'm hopeful—never you mind about that. I'm concerned about your not coming to church."

"You needn't concern yourself with me." He injected as much coolness into his tone as he could manage with her close enough for him to catch her scent of apple blossoms. "The Lord knows the state of my soul."

"Would He be happy with it?"

"Now that is a verra difficult question to answer. But I am thinking the Lord isn't happy with me at all." He turned his back on her and began to fit the glass into the window frame again.

She puffed out a breath. "Colin, you didn't cause your father's death."

"Aye, but there you're wrong. If I'd been with him—"

"You likely would have died, too."

"I might have kept him from going out in a storm."

"So you got your stubbornness from your mother?"

"Ah, Meg—Miss Jordan, you make me laugh, you do." He did laugh, and his soul lightened. "Nay, I got my stubbornness from my father. But if I'd been working with him all along, he wouldn't have felt the need to work too hard and be careless with his life."

"I'm sorry. That's a difficult burden to bear." She moved up beside him, tugged off her gloves, and placed one hand on the glass to steady it in its frame while he applied the caulking. "But you've been forgiven if you've asked for it."

"I ken that's what the Bible tells me, but I don't feel it in my heart." He shifted his position for a better angle, and his hand brushed hers.

Like brushing fine porcelain, creamy and as smooth as her silk glove had been.

He took a deep breath to stop his heart from skipping any more beats than it already had. "I need to bring my family here and keep my work to be truly obedient to the Lord. Just like you're needing to marry that fine gentleman your father wishes you to wed."

"I'm not convinced my father really does wish me to marry Joseph."

Colin dropped his knife. "I beg your pardon?"

"I haven't told anyone, even Sarah, and I probably shouldn't say anything to you." She peeked at him from beneath those extraordinary lashes. "I like talking to you. You listen to me and don't treat me like I'm a child who should run along and play."

"You should, you ken. Perhaps not play but run along."

"That's common sense, but my heart says otherwise. I mean—" She pressed her free hand to her cheek. "By my heart, I mean the feeling I get inside when I see others in need, not my heart in how a lady feels for a—should I stop up my mouth?"

"Aye, probably so." Chuckling, Colin made the mistake of looking at her mouth, those pretty lips that always seemed to curve in a smile. His mouth went dry.

She laughed, too. "I talk too much. You do understand what I'm saying, do you not?"

"I understand." Realizing that he held the caulking knife and was doing nothing with it, he set back to work.

He couldn't avoid looking at her, though. The windowpane reflected her lovely face.

"You want to make me a charity," he made himself say. "Take me in and pamper me like one of your kittens, or teach me American history like the charcoal burners' children."

His words hurt her. He read it in the way her face stilled and her body tensed.

"Your father's already doing plenty for me, Miss Jordan." He gentled his tone. "I have no need of your help."

"What if I could get your family here faster? Would that help you to—to feel worthy of the Lord's love and forgiveness?"

"You're a kind lady, Margaret Jordan."

So kind, so pretty, so giving, he feared he was more than half in love with her.

"But I have to do this myself. 'Tis the only way I can make up for letting them down."

"You can never make up for letting them down, Colin." She placed a bit of emphasis on his Christian name, an emphasis of her defiance of convention, like talking to him at all was. "We can't make up for any of our mistakes, no matter what we do. That's what God's forgiveness is all about."

"I have to try." He finished with the pane but couldn't place the next one with her standing between him and the frame. "I've been given so much. A runaway lad of twelve years should not have found a place in the Edinburgh glassworks, but I did. They needed assistants to carry the molten glass to the glassblowers, and I was quick. I fell in love with the craft and persuaded the master glassblower to teach me." He faced her instead of her reflection. "I have the gift for it. I have to use it to make up for what learning of that gift stole from my family. You ken? I have to do it."

"I don't agree with you, but I understand. I was away at school when my mother died. I didn't want to be there, but Father wouldn't let me come home. That's partly why this school is so important to me. If it works out, children won't have to leave home to get an education. And children from families without the means to pay for boarding school will have an equal opportunity."

"You're a fine lass." Colin stooped to retrieve another pane of glass. "Thaddeus Dalbow warned me to stay away from you if I wish to keep my employment."

"Thaddeus Dalbow tried to kiss me when he was eighteen and I sixteen." She laughed. "We were friends before that, and he got some notions. Father sent him packing with a flea in his ear."

"But your father doesn't like you being too friendly with the workers," Colin said, still selecting glass from the box on the ground.

"No, but—" She sighed. "He doesn't think it good to possibly play favorites. On the other hand, he is already showing you favoritism, and besides that, Ilse Weber is our housekeeper. She raised me after Momma died. I never talk to her husband because I never see him, but I have few secrets from her, and I'm sure she tells him."

"It makes no difference." He rose, holding the glass between them like a shield, while a wild notion formed in his brain, a spark of hope ignited in his heart. "Will you be asking your father if he cares if you talk to me when we meet up?"

"I—could." She looked dubious.

"If you're thinking he'd say no, then get yourself home now. But if 'tis otherwise, I—" He met her eyes, hoping his look conveyed what he dared not say.

Her heightened color suggested she knew exactly what he was saying—she brought sunshine and warmth into his life, and he cared for her more than he should.

"I'm staying to help you finish." She took the glass from his hands. "It's my school. Now show me how to fit this into the frame."

He showed her. With her assistance the work sped by. With time together their conversation grew lighter. As he had the day she stopped to fish with him, he talked to her more in the next hour than he had talked to anyone in the past week. Talking felt like a gift. Listening to her lively way of speaking, gathering the words in his memory felt like treasures he could take out and appreciate in the long hours after work ended for the day and he returned to his empty cottage.

When the work was finished, however, no excuses remained for either of them to stay. Besides, clouds were blowing in from the east, bringing the scent of rain on a chilling breeze.

"We'd best be on our way." He picked up the box the glass had been in and turned to the road without taking a step in that direction.

"I know. I don't want to get my dress soaked in the rain." A stronger gust of wind caught the frill at the bottom of her skirt, and she flattened her hands against the fabric to hold it in place. "Do you have enough provisions to make yourself a fine Sunday dinner?"

"Martha Dalbow sees to my meals. She's a fair good cook."

"That's good then. I worried you weren't eating well."

"You cannot be worrying about me, Miss—Meg."

She wrinkled her nose. "You can't stop me."

"Nay, I have no doubt few people can make you do anything you do not wish to do."

"I expect I'm spoiled."

A blast of wind bearing moisture slammed into their faces.

"We'd better run." Instead of heading to the road, though, she darted around the end of the building. "Leave that box in here." She produced a key from her reticule and unlocked the door. "You can go faster."

"Aye and the straw won't get wet." He dropped the container inside the building, waited for her to lock the door, then left for the road, being careful to measure his longer strides to her shorter ones.

"I knew the fine weather this morning lasted longer than we deserved in December." She sounded breathless but refused to slow down.

They rounded the curve to the intersection. Already

the burn roared louder than when he'd passed it earlier, testimony of rain upstream. Above them the tree branches creaked and groaned, and the lightning-struck tree where he'd first seen her leaned more precariously over the water.

And a bundle of black-and-white fur clung to one of the whipping branches.

"The foolish beastie!" Colin shouted above the wind. "He'll be blown down."

"I don't know how something so small can travel so far. It must be like us walking twenty miles and climbing a mountain." She stopped, and her hat blew off her head. Wind caught her hair and sent her curls flying out like banners. She shoved her hair behind her ears. "We can't just leave him there."

"We should, but, nay, we cannot." Not liking the idea of climbing the unstable tree, Colin began to remove his coat.

"Wait, let's call him first." She laid her hand on his arm then did not remove it when she began to call, "Here, kitty-kitty."

The cat didn't move.

"He's too frightened." Colin removed his arm from her restraining grasp, feeling coldness where her hand had rested. "I'll fetch him. You run along home."

"But what if you fall?"

"I hear a horse. Perhaps 'tis someone who will take you up in a carriage."

"I should go up. I'm lighter."

"Do not dare." He caught the edge of her cloak and found himself holding nothing more than wool.

Meg had slipped out of the garment and darted forward.

"Stubborn braw female," Colin grumbled and sprinted after her.

As Meg set foot on the lowest branch, the kitten leaped from its perch and onto Meg's shoulder. From there it soared to the ground. Colin dove to grab the creature. It slipped past his hands and into the road—right under the hooves of the trotting horse.

ten

Meg screamed and darted for the road. Her flying skirt tangled in her legs, sending her tumbling to the ground. Gravel stung her hands and knees, and the horse's flailing hooves filled her vision.

"I got you." Colin lifted her aside, as though she weighed no more than the kitten, then he lunged past her and bumped his shoulder against the horse's massive flank.

The animal whinnied and leaped aside. The rider shouted a protest.

Dodging another thrashing hoof, Colin snatched up the kitten, then he turned to offer Meg a hand. "Are you all right then, lass?" His fingers were warm, hard, and strong around hers. A firm, reassuring hand with strength enough in the arm to lift her with a gentle tug.

Meg clung to him, swaying a bit and gazing into his face with awe. "You saved my silly kitten."

"And probably crippled my horse." Joseph Pyle stalked toward them, his face red, his blue eyes flashing. "What nonsense were you about, man?"

"Saving the wee beastie for the lady." Colin gave Joseph a gentle smile, though a muscle in his jaw flexed. "Your horse nigh trampled the silly creature."

"And there are ten more where those came from, but there are few finer horses between here and Charleston."

"I would not ken about the horses," Colin said. "But I do ken that Miss Jordan has a fondness for this mite."

"And I have a fondness for—why are you touching her?" If possible, Joseph's face darkened further, making his eyes appear to lose all color in contrast.

Meg met those pale eyes without flinching and gripped Colin's hand more tightly. "I tripped on my skirt and fell, and now he's making sure I'm steady."

And she loved the excuse to hold his hand again.

"Release him." Joseph's words sounded like the bark of an angry dog. "You demean yourself, Margaret."

"I will in a moment." She still felt off balance, light-headed—more from Joseph's words than the fall and close call with the kitten. "A strong hand for support is welcome."

She glanced at Joseph's long, elegant hand clad in a buttery leather glove.

"You may take my arm." He held out the appendage. "I'll walk you home. Grassick, take my horse to my farm."

Meg didn't move. Every fiber in her being rebelled at taking orders from Joseph and against him for giving Colin directives like he was a groom.

Colin didn't stir either, other than to shift his gaze from Joseph to her.

"Have you two lost your hearing?" Joseph demanded.

"I heard you perfectly well, Joseph." Meg worked to keep her tone even.

"Then stop making a fool of yourself and come home before this storm breaks."

"You'd best go, lass." Colin squeezed her fingers and released her hand. "And perhaps take this kitten into the house so he can't wander so far afield." He placed the trembling feline in her hands.

"Thank you. That will have to wait until I'm home again." She cradled the cat against her throat and gave Colin one more glance. She wanted to speak to him, tell him things about herself and God and hopes and anything that came to mind. Nothing seemed possible, even appropriate, in front of Joseph.

"I'm ready to go," she said to Joseph.

"Finally." He held out the reins. "Grassick, I said to take my horse."

Colin still didn't move.

"What's wrong with you?" Joseph's voice went up half an octave.

"Naught is wrong with me, Mr. Pyle." Colin looked at the gelding, whose back was nearly the height of Colin's chin. "'Tis just that I have no knowledge about how to handle a horse."

"You don't know how to handle a horse?" Joseph's surprise seemed genuine. "What sort of man doesn't know how to handle a horse?"

"Joseph," Meg breathed out in protest.

Colin shrugged. "The kind who's never owned one, perhaps. The kind who goes from fishing to glassmaking and has no need of one."

"Huh." Joseph shook his head. "Then just go about your business. Margaret, come with me."

Because she knew it was what her father would want her to do, Meg nodded to Colin with a silent "thank you," took Joseph's arm, and let him lead her on the one side and his mount on the other.

"What were you doing with him?" Joseph demanded before they were quite out of Colin's earshot.

"He was working on replacing the windows in the school. I stopped to talk to him."

Rain began to fall in big, heavy drops. Joseph increased their pace. "He shouldn't be working on a Sunday."

"He volunteered to replace the windows. He isn't getting paid. I think the Lord will accept charitable work on a Sunday."

"Charitable work that gets him in the good graces of the owner's daughter."

Meg slanted a look at Joseph, wondering if he was jealous, then chastised herself for such a vain thought. "He is trying to please the people who sponsored his coming here to find a better life, Joseph. His dedication to his work is commendable, and Father and I are both happy with him."

"A little too happy," Joseph grumbled. "You were holding his hand."

"I told you—"

"It isn't proper," Joseph interrupted. "You're going to marry me."

Not if she could find a way to avoid it.

"You shouldn't encourage his kind."

"His—kind?" Meg released her grip on Joseph's arm. "What do you mean by that?"

"A man without property or prospects."

"I think his prospects are rather good. He has skill and talent and—"

"Not a roof to call his own, let alone hundreds of acres, as I have." The rain grew heavier, and Joseph walked faster still. "But enough of him. I am assured you won't spend any more time with him."

She had given him no such reassurance and didn't intend to.

"I'm pleased I saw you today, even though we didn't have our dinner as usual."

Meg pulled up her hood for protection but said nothing.

"I know I agreed to hold off making our betrothal official until after the first of the year," Joseph said.

The abrupt change of subject threw Meg off balance, and she stammered out a response. "Ye–es, I have a number of things I need to think about between now and then."

"Frivolous things, from all I can see." Joseph's tone grew indulgent. "Your friend's wedding and Christmas."

"And my school."

"Oh, that." He dismissed her hard work with a wave of one hand. "You'll lose interest in that once you start thinking about a wedding and all the things we'll need to furnish our home properly. I want it fine enough to entertain the governor."

Why not the president?

Meg refrained from asking such a flippant question.

"I can afford the best, you know," Joseph continued. "And you have exhibited fine taste in these matters."

"Thank you." Meg caught sight of the lane to her house and nearly broke into a run.

"But I've decided that the delay to our betrothal is unacceptable," Joseph said.

Meg tripped on the smooth road.

"When your father returns from Philadelphia on Tuesday, I intend to tell him that we will announce our betrothal at Sarah and Peter's wedding."

"You will do no such thing." Despite the rain Meg stopped in the middle of the road, placed her free hand on her hip, and glared at him. "Sarah and Peter's wedding is their special day. You will not try to steal attention by making such an announcement."

"When else will we have so many people assembled?" Joseph raised one brow, more bemused than angry. "It's when I want it done."

"It's not when I want it announced." Meg took a deep breath. "If you say anything at the wedding celebration, I will—will—I'll denounce you."

"You wouldn't dare," Joseph said through his teeth. "If I say it's so, you will go along with me."

"I won't." Meg took a step backward. Her heart raced, and breathing seemed difficult. "You can't make me."

She didn't care if she sounded childish. She felt like a child—a child frightened of the dark, when she was a woman afraid of the man not a yard away from her.

"In truth I don't ever want our betrothal announced." Turning on her heel, she gathered up her skirt and broke into a trot.

"Margaret, stop this nonsense." Joseph's feet pounded in the forming mud, the horse's hooves clomping along with him.

She kept going.

He grabbed her arm, spun her toward him. "Don't you

ever run away from me again. I have paid for your father's permission to court you."

"But not to treat me roughly." She tried to pull free.

Paid for? She would think about the meaning of his remark later.

"I want to go home. I'm cold and wet."

"You should have thought of that before you started flirting with that glassblower."

"I wasn't—" No, she would not defend herself or her friendship with Colin. "Let go of me, Joseph."

"I will when I deliver you to the Thompsons' front door." He gripped her arm, not quite hard enough to hurt but harder than she liked, too hard for her to get free without a struggle.

She couldn't struggle against him, but she needed to get away. She made herself go still. Around her, the rain drummed so hard it sounded like footfalls racing toward them.

It was footfalls. They pounded harder than the rain. Meg twisted around and saw Colin dash up to them, grasp Joseph's wrist, and break his hold.

"The lass said to let go of her." His green eyes glowed like sea fire.

A shiver that had nothing to do with the cold rain raced through Meg. The gelding tossed his head and sidled away from the two men, and Joseph stood, his hair and face shining in the downpour, as though turned into a glass sculpture.

"Verra good." Colin smiled and released Joseph's arm. "If you like, Miss Jordan, I'll escort you the rest of the way to Miss Thompson's house."

"Th—thank you." Meg clenched her teeth to keep them from chattering. "I w—would like that."

"I wouldn't go anywhere with him if I were you." Joseph's voice was as cold as the rain. "You won't like the consequences to your father."

Meg stared at him. "Is that a threat?"

Joseph merely smiled.

Colin curled his fingers around Meg's elbow. "We must get you out of this weather."

Without so much as a nod in Joseph's direction, Colin urged Meg back to the road and toward the Thompson farm. Rain splashed and pounded around them. The road turned to a river of mud. But no thud of hooves resounded behind them. Once Meg glanced back. She spotted no sign of Joseph.

"On horseback he can ride across the fields to his house faster than taking the road," she observed.

"I expect he has." Colin's mouth was set in a grim line. "'Twould be against his pride to follow us after you set your preference for my escort."

"That was probably unwise of me, wasn't it?"

"Aye, probably so." Light pressure on her elbow took the sting from his agreement.

Meg's throat closed. "Do you think he can harm you? I mean, can he make Father dismiss you?"

"Can he harm me? Aye. Can he persuade your father to dismiss me?" Colin said nothing more until they reached Sarah's drive. There he paused beneath the protective canopy of an ancient pine and faced her. "If Joseph Pyle can persuade your father that you should marry him, when 'tis against your wishes, I'm thinking he can persuade your father to make an unwise business decision like dismissing me."

"Colin." Meg pressed her hand to her lips. "You think Joseph has some sort of—control over my father?"

"I'm thinking a father who provides his daughter with a school with fine glass in the windows, a man who lets his daughter bring home stray cats and lets her go fishing with a glassblower is not verra likely to insist she wed a man she does not like."

"Are you saying"—she clutched at his arm—"that Joseph

is somehow forcing Father to go along with his wishes?"

"I cannot say anything so bold as all that." He covered her hand with his. "But I'm saying I think some things aren't right, you ken?"

"I know." Meg blinked back tears. "What should I do?"

"Mr. Pyle has a fancy for you and will treat you well when not having his pride pricked, so I'm saying you should go along with your father's wishes and accept his proposal." He turned over his injured left hand. "And when I can work again, I'll make you a fine gift to display in your new home."

She felt as though Joseph's gelding had kicked in her chest, crushing her heart. "You're telling me to marry another man?"

"Aye, that I am." Colin's face was stiff. "I am not worth you having to choose between obeying your father and even being friends with me."

"You are." She could only speak in a whisper.

He gave her a smile though his eyes were sad. "And I cannot put my own wishes before my family another time. I do not feel I have the forgiveness once, let alone twice."

More protests crowded into her throat, but she held them back. She would do everything she could to stop her impending betrothal to Joseph, but she could not compromise Colin's position at the glassworks and his family's better future.

"We'd better get into the house before we both catch a chill." She turned toward the lane. "Come into the kitchen. There'll be something hot to drink and a warm fire where you can dry yourself."

They didn't speak until they reached the walk of flagstones leading to the front door. Colin tried to wish her good-bye there, but she insisted on accompanying him all the way around the house to the kitchen door. The Thompsons' housekeeper greeted them with exclamations over their bedraggled state and sent her daughter running to fetch Sarah.

"We've been worried about you," the housekeeper said. "Sarah thought you would be here long before now."

"I'm sorry." Meg drew Colin to stand beside her at the fire. "One of my kittens—oh." She stuck her hand into her pocket, where the kitten lay curled up and soaked. "Poor thing. I forgot about him. Colin, will you be so kind as to take it to the stable on your way home?"

"Of course." He smiled at Meg, their eyes meeting and holding, as their hands touched in the exchange. "Perhaps this experience will teach him to stop wandering quite so much."

"I think so." She kept her fingers touching his hand. "Feel his little heart. It's beating like a parade drum."

"Aye, I ken how he feels." Colin smiled and drew his hand away. "Now run along with your friend and get yourself dry. This fine lady is making cups of tea, and Miss Thompson is waiting for you."

Meg nodded and turned her back on him, her own heart sinking to her toes.

Sarah stood in the doorway, silent, staring. As soon as Meg faced her, she spun on her heel and marched out of the kitchen. Meg followed. Neither of them spoke until they reached Sarah's bedchamber on the second floor.

"Margaret Jordan, whatever are you thinking?" Sarah sounded out of breath.

Meg removed her sodden cloak and shoes before answering. "I'm thinking that I don't want to marry Joseph even though I know it's for the best that I do."

"That's what I was afraid you'd say when I witnessed that touching scene down there." Sarah pressed her hands to her cheeks. "You're in love with him, aren't you? The glassblower, I mean."

Without needing even a moment to think of her response, Meg nodded. "Yes, I'm in love with him. But if I don't marry Joseph, it could ruin Colin's life and possibly my father's, too."

eleven

Colin spent the evening writing letters to his family. He needed to see each name, conjure every face in his head to remind him of his purpose for being in America, in sending Meg on her way. All for the sake of his family. He could risk nothing that would prevent him from bringing his family to America, where a home to live, a place for them to get an education, the opportunity to have better lives spread out before them.

"This land is vast," he wrote. "People speak of New Jersey being too crowded, but if this is crowded, I cannot imagine the emptiness of the lands beyond the mountains."

Nor the abundance of the fish in the lochs he'd heard of to the west and north, lochs big enough to be seas. He wrote of all of it to his family then set the missive aside for when Mr. Jordan returned. His employer had already promised he would help transfer money to Colin's family, using his agent in England.

Writing to his family, knowing the money would ease their lot a bit lessened Colin's distress. He had a fine home, warmth, and plenty to eat. He was even making friends, thanks to the Dalbows' warmth and hospitality. Yet his heart ached with every thought of Meg that crept into his head, and in the dark quiet of night, he wished he'd stayed in Edinburgh, though the opportunities to help his family had been too few to count in the crowded, expensive city.

"Haven't I suffered enough, Lord?" he cried out in his empty house. "What else will I have to do to prove I've reformed my ways and am now devoted to my family?"

With his hand injured, he was losing wages. A body

couldn't be a master glassblower with the use of only one hand. He needed both to balance the pipe and manipulate the glass. He could manage some drawings, so he stood at a table beneath the windows and began to think of objects he could make for Meg as a wedding present from the glassworks' employees. He considered a vase, but that was too easy, too common, and her friend's fiancé had commissioned a pair of them for his new bride. The same went for candlesticks. She would get plenty of those for wedding gifts. This had to be special, perhaps useless. . .or perhaps simply frivolous.

He chewed on his pencil and gazed out the window, thinking of things he could make, thinking of things Meg could use. Thinking of Meg—her smooth hands, her bright smile, her scent of apple blossoms even in the winter.

Scent—of course. She must wear some sort of scent. He could make her a scent bottle, something delicate yet sturdy, bright and effervescent like Meg herself.

"How's your hand?" Thad joined Colin at the window.

"It's all right." Colin frowned at the blisters. They were healing well. "But I have too much work to be woolgathering here by the windows."

"You can't work with that hand though." Thad leaned toward the windows. "I see the finches have brought some friends. They like the warmth, and Martha sprinkles a bit of grain for them."

"They're not verra attractive birds." Colin eyed the cluster of tiny finches gathered in the yard.

They were a dull brown, but lively and talkative among one another.

"The males turn a bright yellow in the spring," Thad explained. "Martha is convinced they have the same spouses year after year, too. I don't care much for birds unless they're in the cooking pot, but Martha likes them."

Colin studied the finches picking at the ground with

their pointed, pink beaks. They were small, not more than four inches long, but their vivacity whirled around them.

"They'll be a fine sight when they're in their courting feathers." Colin grasped his pencil and began to draw.

Thad stood and watched. "That's how you advanced so fast in Edinburgh. You can design, too."

"Aye, I had a good teacher." Colin hesitated, then he changed the bird's position so that it was launching into flight, its beak pointing skyward. "Do you think 'twill do for a perfume bottle? The beak can be the stopper."

"A perfume bottle, eh?" Thad studied the design. "We've made medicine bottles aplenty here. They're easy but nothing as fancy as this. Do you think ladies would buy it?"

"'Tis not for sale. 'Tis intended as a gift."

"I see." Thad glanced toward the desk, where a box of the purple goblets rested, and Colin understood that Thad saw a great deal.

Neither Colin nor Meg had tried to hide their growing feelings for each other. Inspecting the blisters on his left hand, Colin wondered—not for the first time—if someone had noticed, disapproved, and thought of a way to be rid of Colin without doing him in—just preventing him from working, perhaps long enough to get him dismissed.

"You did not succeed," Colin muttered.

"What was that?" Thad asked.

"I was talking to myself. Is there aught I can do?"

"Carry those glasses to the Jordans' house." Thad started back to his bench. "Miss Jordan has taken it into her head to learn to knit. She's over there having Martha teach her right now."

The message was clear—Meg wouldn't be at home, so going to the Jordans' was safe.

She wasn't home; she was walking around the end of the glassworks as Colin left with the glasses. He couldn't avoid her without being rude, and his heart cried out to God, protesting the encounter at the same time it thrilled at the sight of her.

"Peter and Sarah are coming to fetch me," she told him. "It's not raining or snowing, so I thought I'd walk to the end of the drive. I won't get another chance to walk for another two days at the least, and I do love to—" She broke off and giggled. "I'm talking too much, aren't I?"

"Aye, that you are." Colin grinned at her. "But I like the sound of your voice."

"No no, you're the one with the fine voice. It's"—she tilted her head and smiled up at him—"musical."

"You flatter me." He looked away from her so he could regain his composure. "Shall I escort you to the gate, Miss Jordan?"

She took a step closer to him. "I was Meg yesterday."

"You should not have been." He adjusted his grip on the box. "Perhaps I should be delivering this half of your wedding present to your house, as Thad told me to."

"There will be no wedding." Meg spoke through her teeth. "Tomorrow, when my father returns home, I will tell him absolutely I will not marry Joseph Pyle."

"You do as you think is right, but you will still have to be Miss Jordan to me."

"I don't want—"

The ringing of the gate bell interrupted her.

"Good day." Colin inclined his head and headed toward the side gate that led to the fields of the Jordan farm, a rough shortcut to the house. Behind him, he heard Meg make a noise, something like a sob. He refused to look back. He'd be doomed if he did. A man only had so much strength for resisting even a few minutes with the lady he loved.

≈

While hunting up work to keep himself occupied, from sweeping up the cullet off the floor, to nailing crates together for Meg to use as benches in her school, Colin prayed for no more encounters with Meg. That another errand took him into her presence again the following morning proved to him how little God paid attention to him. He was still doing wrong in the Lord's eyes.

If only the Thompsons had waited another day to ask for someone from the glassworks to measure the globes in their sconces to make some replacements, Meg would have been back home. Instead she perched on the edge of a sofa, snippets of white yarn sticking to her dress like snowflakes, while she counted stitches on a knitting needle in the room into which Mrs. Thompson led him.

"I don't know how I ended up with thirty-four stitches, when I started out with thirty. Martha warned me about dropping stitches but—" She stopped talking to her friend Sarah, and pink tinged her cheeks.

"I beg your pardon, ladies." He bowed his head and tried to turn his back on Meg so he could concentrate on the business at hand—the measurement of a sconce globe made of glass that was far too dark to be of much use.

"Did you knit two stitches from the same loop?" Sarah asked a little too loudly.

"Did I what?" Meg sounded vague.

Colin smiled and took out his caliper to measure the base and height of the globe.

"Are you going to replace the glass, Mrs. Thompson?" Meg asked.

"I was thinking of it," Mrs. Thompson said. "The glass in these is so gray the candlelight doesn't show through very well."

"Will you use flint glass to make them, um, Mr. Grassick?" Meg's voice emerged breathless.

Colin glanced over his shoulder at her and smiled. The sight of her with her hair in loose curls tumbling down her back, confined only by a blue velvet ribbon, the white wool yarn in her hands stole his breath, robbed him of anything sensible beyond the ability to nod.

"Maybe Sarah and I can come watch you work one day." Meg smiled. "I've seen them make the windows, but something like these globes is much more interesting."

"If Mr. Jordan says 'tis all right, I'd be honored." He made himself turn to Mrs. Thompson. "Is there anything else, ma'am?"

"No." She drew out the single word, and her hazel eyes flitted between him and Meg. "Send us the estimate on the cost of four globes for this room as soon as you can."

"Aye, er, yes, ma'am." As he exited the room, he allowed himself one more look at Meg, met and held her gaze for a moment longer than necessary. A moment longer than was good for his heart.

Outside, a blast of cold, damp air slapped him in the face along with the sight of Joseph Pyle riding up on his fine chestnut horse. Pyle, who had a right to call on Meg.

Colin returned to the glassworks, where he assisted one of the other workers to break some rather well-done bowls out of the new molds. They lacked the artistry of blown glass pieces, but they were also far cheaper.

In the early afternoon Colin returned to his cottage for his dinner and found Meg placing a basket on his back stoop.

"I do not think you should be here, Miss Jordan." He made his posture and manner as formal as he knew how.

She tossed her head back. "Martha Dalbow is right next door, and I was just leaving this here. Mrs. Weber made dinner for Father, but he didn't come home, so I brought it over to you."

"And I'm an ungrateful beast for not thanking you. But, my dear—I mean, Miss Jordan—"

"I prefer 'my dear.'" She took a step closer to him, one hand outstretched. "Colin—"

Footfalls sounded on the gravel path between the cottages, and Meg's face paled. Colin knew what—or who—he would see even before Meg spoke.

"Father, you're home at last. And, Mr. Pyle, good afternoon."

"Run along home, Margaret," Jordan said. "Joseph will escort you. Grassick, shall we go inside your house and talk?"

"Aye, sir." Without so much as a glance in Meg's direction, Colin picked up the basket she had carried with her own soft hands to his doorstep, and he opened the door.

The cottage was cold. Colin made haste to build up the fire from the banked coals and set a kettle of water on for tea. Purring, the cat rubbed around his ankles.

Jordan arrived in a few moments and closed the door. He didn't sit; he stood with his back to the panels, his arms folded across his chest. "How's the hand?"

Colin started at the question, expecting something quite different. "It's healing nicely, sir. I should be back to work shortly. In the meantime I'm making myself as useful as possible."

"Good. We have a number of new orders from my journey to Philadelphia." Jordan cleared his throat. "The others are learning finer work from you, but they aren't up to your standards and won't be for a long time. You know all this, and I reiterate it to emphasize how much I need you."

Colin said nothing. He sensed Jordan intended to say more—more Colin wouldn't like.

"However," Jordan continued, "Pyle tells me you've been annoying my daughter."

Colin stiffened. "Nay, sir, I would not call it annoying."

"Neither would I, which is the difficulty." Jordan sighed, and his arms dropped to his sides. "Margaret enjoys your company. That's all too apparent, and it cannot continue. To secure my daughter's future, I must tell you that if this friendship between you continues, I will have to discharge you."

twelve

"You disappoint me, Margaret." Father spoke from the head of the dining room table as Meg poured the after-supper coffee. "I thought you'd be too occupied helping Sarah with her wedding, and now I understand you've spent half your time with a glassblower."

"You exaggerate, Father." Meg softened her words with a smile. "Only a wee bit of my time, all told."

"Any time is too much." Father's frown warned her not to speak with haste. "You know how I feel about your being friendly with the workers, but you've been at the Dalbows' and today were standing outside Grassick's cottage talking to him. The impropriety shames me and should shame you, too."

Meg set down the coffeepot before she dropped it and clutched the back of her chair. "I am ashamed of nothing I've done, sir. Mr. Grassick is a kind, Christian man who has behaved with utmost propriety whenever in my company."

"And Joseph tells me you continue to rebuff his attentions." Father spoke as though she had said nothing. "Why?"

"I've made that clear, Father. I don't wish to marry him."

"But I want you to." His tone gentled. "My dear, I need to see your future secure, for my peace of mind."

"Father?" Meg rushed to his side. "You're not ill, are you? Please, tell me you're not ill. Did you go to Philadelphia to see a physician? Father—"

"Hush." He caressed her cheek. "I'm fit as a fiddle. But I wasn't a young man when I married your mother, and we must all face our mortality one day. I want this farm and the glassworks in the hands of a man who can see them prosper and regain the investment I've made to get the glassworks going again. Your mother said I shouldn't start up until I had saved enough to remain debt free, but I broke that promise in my grief and borrowed too much money. So we need someone who can keep the glassworks building profits. Joseph is that man."

And Colin wasn't. Father didn't need to say so for Meg to understand this. He knew nothing of farming. Colin was a fine artisan, but he had never managed a business, didn't know about sales and accounts and bankers. She knew how to run a household and cook a fine meal, sew a nearly invisible seam and almost knit, but no one had taught her more management skills than being wise with the household accounts. Too many people depended on them for their livelihoods to entrust the land to inexperienced persons.

"Please, Father, not yet." She sank to her knees and laid her cheek against his arm as she had as a child. "Give me time to learn. I did well with my sums. I can learn. Many women run their own farms and businesses, too."

Father patted her on the head. "I'll try to keep him from pushing his suit until after the first of the year as I promised, daughter, but Joseph is a man who goes after what he wants with fervor. Right now, he wants two things—you as his wife and repayment of the money I borrowed from him. Now, let us go into the parlor and read some scripture."

She chose Colossians and stumbled over the third chapter. "If ye then be risen with Christ, seek those things which are above, where Christ sitteth on the right hand of God. Set your affection on things above, not on things on the earth." Then the later verses about obedience to one's parents being pleasing to God.

She wanted to agree to marry Joseph, even let him announce their betrothal at Sarah's wedding, but because her heart rebelled, she could say nothing. If she kept herself occupied, she didn't need to think about it and nearly managed not to think about Colin.

Occupation was easy with the wedding three days off. A local seamstress had made Meg's gown, but she needed to finish the embroidery around the neck and hem. She and Sarah helped make pastries and breads and peel mounds of potatoes for the fifty guests who would enjoy a buffet at the Thompsons' after the ceremony. She spent the night at the Thompson house so she could assist Sarah in washing, curling, and pinning up her heavy auburn tresses.

At last Sarah, quiet but smiling, glowing in her pink velvet gown, stood ready to go to the church. Her female cousins surrounded her in their own velvet dresses, like a pastel flower garden of primrose, lilac, and pale blue.

Meg had chosen a darker blue for her own gown and stitched the neck and hem with tiny white roses. She wore white silk roses in her hair. Everyone told her she looked stunning. She didn't once glance in a mirror to verify the truth of their words. Her looks didn't matter.

As quiet as Sarah, Meg climbed into the carriage Father had sent over to fetch her, and she managed not to sigh with disappointment when she saw Joseph sitting beside her parent.

"Next winter," Joseph said, "I'll buy you a fur-lined cloak."

Meg clenched her hands together inside her muff. "I'm quite warm enough in this one, thank you."

But if he was her husband, she couldn't stop him from buying anything he liked. Nor, since he was the man her father had chosen for her, could she stop him from escorting her into the church for the ceremony. She could, however, ignore him as Sarah and Peter exchanged their vows, their faces glowing brighter than the candles massed along the altar to counteract the gloom of a winter day.

Meg's eyes dimmed and blurred with tears. She wanted that kind of love. She rejoiced for her friend, but her heart ached.

When she stood and turned to go at the end of the service, she caught a glimpse of sunset red hair at the back of the sanctuary. Her heart constricted. With all her will, she stopped herself from pushing through the throng of the congregation to join Colin at the back. But no will in the world stopped the prayer she sent to the Lord, asking, pleading, begging Him to change her circumstances. She then took Joseph's proffered arm to exit the church. When she reached the benches at the rear of the church, Colin was gone.

Outside, snow fell like sugar crystals to ice the ground. Ladies paused to strap on the wooden pattens that added inches to their height and kept their light slippers and long dresses dry. Meg clung to Joseph's arm then to keep her balance and received the warmest smile he'd ever bestowed upon her.

"Peter may be the luckiest man today," Joseph said, "but I'm surely the second luckiest to have you on my arm."

"They look so happy." Meg sighed. "And Sarah is beautiful."

"You're even prettier." Joseph patted her hand. "How did you get such a pretty daughter, Jordan?"

Father laughed. "Her mother."

"Guessed as much." Joseph nodded to the line of carriages and horses heading to the Thompson house. "How will they manage all these vehicles?"

"They hired extra men from around the county," Father explained. "It won't be easy with all the snow."

"That's why I'm willing to wait for a spring wedding." Joseph patted a lock of his hair away from his brow. "One runs the risk of mud, but it's not as bad as snow. And I do like to think of Margaret in silk. Pale blue silk. I'll buy a bolt when I'm in New York the week after Christmas."

"You mustn't," Meg cried. "That's far too much."

"No no, it's not beyond my budget." Joseph chuckled. "Nor is a fine wedding."

"I will pay for my daughter's wedding." Father's voice

turned as frosty as the air.

Meg gritted her teeth.

"Will there be dancing tonight?" Joseph asked.

"No, the house isn't big enough." Meg caught a glimpse of the house, ablaze with light and bursting with guests, and smiled. "But there is music."

"Too bad." Joseph prepared to exit the carriage first. "I did want to dance with you, Margaret, and I'll be gone for the Christmas party."

"That's unfortunate for you."

The carriage stopped. Joseph alighted and assisted Meg to the ground then led her inside. Warmth and noise and the aromas of roasting meats and candied fruits greeted them. Meg managed to elude Joseph long enough to take her cloak to an upstairs bedchamber and tuck a few pins more securely into her hair. Once downstairs, she found Sarah and Peter and hugged them both.

"It'll be you next," Sarah said.

Meg merely smiled and turned to greet some neighbors who lived farther away and usually attended a different church.

"When are you getting married?" two matrons asked her in succession.

"When I find a man who loves me like Peter loves Sarah," she responded.

"You young girls read too many novels, to have those kinds of notions." An elderly lady patted Meg's cheek. "You want a man who can provide you with a good home and fine children."

"Yes, ma'am." She smiled and agreed until her face hurt, and all the while she wished Colin stood beside her, his hand tucked into the crook of her arm as Peter held Sarah close to his side. She would smile up at him and let everyone see how much she loved him—

"I've brought you a plate of food." Joseph stood in front of her bearing two laden plates. "Come. There's a table here in the dining room, where we can be comfortable. I paid one of the servants to keep it empty for us."

Martha Dalbow, in her Sunday best, guarded the two places. She smiled at Meg then darted away to pick up an empty serving plate.

"Martha isn't a servant." Meg seated herself in the chair Joseph pulled out. "She's my friend."

"If she were your friend," Joseph drawled, "she would be sitting at the table, not waiting on it."

Meg closed her eyes and prayed for a still tongue.

"Aren't you going to eat?" Joseph asked. "The food is good. Plain but good. When we get married—"

"Will you please excuse me." Feeling so hot she couldn't breathe, Meg pushed back her chair. She rose and exited the room before Joseph managed to stand.

The house wasn't big enough nor the crowd dense enough for her to hide from him. So she kept going through the parlor, into the entryway, and out the front door. The blast of snow-laden air cleared her head instantly. She stood on the porch for a moment, breathing in gulps of clear air; then, hearing the scrape of shovels on the flagstones of the walk, she descended the steps and walked into the darkness of the yard, heedless of snow soaking into her shoes. She wouldn't be there for long, just enough to regain her composure and set her roiling stomach to rights.

She heard no footfalls on the white carpet, but when a hand curved over her shoulder, she neither jumped nor cried out. A scent, a touch, or perhaps pure instinct told her who stood behind her before he spoke.

"Are you all right then, lass?"

"I am now." She rested her head against his shoulder. "But why are you here?"

"I'm helping out with the snow shoveling."

"What about your hand?"

"'Tis all right." For a moment he rested his cheek atop her head. "What drove you into the snow?"

"It was hot and noisy inside, and everyone kept asking me when I'm going to get married. And Joseph keeps talking about how much better our wedding will be than Sarah and Peter's."

"I expect it will be." He lowered his hand from her shoulder but didn't move away from her. "If you marry him, that is."

"If? I don't see that I have a choice."

"I wish it weren't so."

"Me, too. I just wish—I wish I knew why he is so determined to marry me."

"'Tis simple for me to understand." Tenderness infused his tone. "He wants to be an important man. To him, that means having possessions he can show off. And you, lass, are a wife to show off."

"I'm not an ornament." She shuddered.

"Well, having you on one's arm would do a man's pride good." He sounded as though he smiled. "What concerns me about Mr. Pyle is the lengths to which he will go to get what he wants."

Meg gasped. "What are you saying?"

"Naught for which I have the proof." His accent thickened. "But if I did, I would be standing up in the kirk to denounce his right to wed you."

"Colin, you couldn't. You could lose your position at the glassworks. Your family would suffer if you angered him and Father."

"Aye, they might, but what about you suffering if I have the knowledge and do naught about it?"

"Do you know something?" She clenched her fists. "If so, tell me."

"I'm gathering the proof first, lass. Meanwhile, try not to announce your marriage. Unless—" Frost tinged his voice. "Unless you want to marry an important man."

"You know I don't want to be important," Meg cried. "I want to be loved."

Someone opened the door of the house, and fiddle music and laughter danced into the night. Then the door closed. The music ceased.

In the ensuing stillness Colin murmured, "You are, lass. You are most certainly loved."

She straightened, turned, faced him. "Colin, I lo—"

"Nay." He pressed a finger to her lips. "Do not say it until you're certain you will not wed the man."

"You know I must. Father—Colin, I'm afraid Joseph is using Father's debt to him to force this marriage."

"Aye, it seems likely, and 'tis a good reason why you should not wed the man."

"What do you know?"

"I do not ken for certain, but one cannot help but overhear bits of conversation from time to time. It seems Pyle loaned your father money to restart the glassworks," Colin explained, "and now the note is due without the profit to pay it yet."

"And I'm payment for the debt." Despite the crisp, clear air, Meg could scarcely breathe. "I can take care of my own future, but I don't know what Father would do without the glassworks or maybe even the farm."

"Aye, which is why I am hoping I'm wrong in thinking what I am of Joseph Pyle, if you will wed him."

"I can't abandon the needs of my father any more than you can abandon the needs of your family."

"I'll do my best to change things. There must be a way out."

"If there were, I'd take it."

Colin's chest rose and fell in a silent sigh. "You should go back inside before you catch a chill." He brushed snow from her hair then let his fingertips linger against her cheek.

She didn't move. She feared even a breath would dislodge his hand from her face, would send her skittering across the snowy grass in an opposite direction to his. If she remained motionless, the moment would last as long as she wanted it to. There in the night, a gauzy curtain of snow sheltered them from the music and laughter in the house, where half a hundred people celebrated someone else's wedding.

"I can't go in there." Meg clasped his hand against her face. "I can't go back there and pretend I'm happy. I want to stay out here with you, where I don't have to pretend."

"Aye, lass, the pretending lies in thinking we don't have to say good-bye." He curved his other hand beneath her chin. "Or that I have a right to this."

He touched his lips to hers. His kiss was warm and gentle and far too brief. Before her heart remembered to beat, before she thought to respond, he drew his hands away from her face, turned his back on her, and vanished behind the swirling mantle of snow.

thirteen

Meg decided to set up a Christmas party to introduce her school to the county. She could serve hot cider and coffee and little cakes and give the children some sort of gift, like a bag of sweets. The planning would keep her occupied, would steer her mind away from thoughts of Colin, of the kiss, of his walking away from her because she insisted she must marry Joseph for everyone's sake. Activity must fill up the empty place in her heart.

Christmas lay three weeks off, and Father and she always entertained on Christmas Eve. She must plan for that, too, not to mention help Ilse clean and cook and decorate the house with evergreen boughs and holly berries. But no mistletoe this year. Meg wouldn't risk Joseph coming across her standing beneath it. After Colin's kiss, she never wanted another man to so much as touch her hand.

Colin had kissed her.

Meg paused in the middle of the planning that was supposed to make her forget, and she pressed her fingertips to her lips, as though the gesture could seal in the memory of that all-too-brief contact. He had held her face as tenderly as a blown glass ornament.

"I love you, too," she whispered.

No answer returned from the four walls of her bedchamber. Beyond the windows the world lay in white silence. They would need the sleigh to get to church.

She hurried to dress and descend to make breakfast. Father came in the door as Meg finished toasting slices of bread. Snow clung to his hair in streaks of white, making him look ten years older until the flakes melted from the kitchen's warmth in moments. Those were enough moments to give Meg a pang of apprehension, a reminder that Father, although not old, was certainly no longer young.

"I should have come out to help you," she said.

"No need. We got the sleigh out yesterday when the sky grew so dark. But that coffee won't go amiss." He seated himself at the table.

Meg served him coffee, toast, and eggs then seated herself. "It's early for so much snow."

"A bit." Father spread apple butter on his toast. "Where did you disappear to last night?"

"I needed some air." Meg stared at her plate, the food untouched. "I'm going to miss Sarah."

"She's only a mile farther up the road."

"Yes, but it won't be the same, will it? I mean with her married and me—" Too late she realized her error.

"You can be married, too." Father wasn't eating either, though he held his toast. "When Joseph asks you again, you will accept."

"Yes, Father."

She knew she must, for her father's sake, for Colin's sake. She mustn't let Joseph have the right to take over the glassworks, or then Colin would lose his position and his family would remain in a tiny, damp, and drafty cottage without enough fuel to burn or food to eat.

Father relaxed. "I'm glad to see you've gotten sense about this."

"Yes, Father."

Sense enough to pray that Joseph would not ask her. For surely this was not God's will for her life, especially if Colin was right. God didn't want her to spend money on fine furnishings so they could entertain the governor. God wanted her to open her school and knit mufflers for the children, aid the poor with soup and blankets, and make sweets for the church's spring fete. Surely God wouldn't give her a man she loved and one who loved her, only to tear them apart. God would never expect her to sacrifice her happiness for the sake of a man's greed and desire to possess things.

"I just wish," she ventured, "that Joseph weren't so interested in owning things."

"He was raised that way." Father buttered more toast. "His father made a great deal of money as a privateer during the Revolution. But he didn't live very long to enjoy it."

"That's very sad." Meg rose. "I'll go fetch the lap robes from the linen press. We'll need them with this cold." She hesitated in the doorway. "I've decided to open the school early, as a sort of Christmas present to the local children. A week from tomorrow. I'll have a bit of a party. Is that all right with you?"

"Yes, daughter, it'll keep your mind off Sarah being away." Father gave her an indulgent smile.

Strength flowing back into her limbs, Meg raced upstairs to collect the heavy rugs they used to keep themselves warm in the sleigh. She could start with her school. She could concentrate on the children and not think about Colin or Joseph.

Not thinking of either of them at church proved impossible. Joseph sat beside her in the Jordan pew rather than alone in his own family section, and Colin sat in the back. She exchanged pleasantries with Joseph, giving him an invitation to dinner, and turned as soon as the service ended in order to catch the merest glimpse of Colin.

With his height and bright hair, he stood out in the crowd, standing beside Martha and Thad Dalbow—and what appeared to be half a dozen young women surrounded him, fluttering their lashes and making their side curls bob against rosy cheeks. In response he smiled and turned a reddish hue that clashed with his hair.

Meg laughed. Seeing him with friends and well made her smile. His discomfiture over the female attention amused her.

"I'm pleased your father told him to stop annoying you," Joseph said beside her. "He appears to get enough female attention without demanding yours."

"He never demanded it, Joseph. He has a kind and gentle spirit."

Joseph snorted. "Which is why he's working for someone else."

Meg swung around to stare at Joseph, sharp words burning on her tongue. A group of neighbors wanting to discuss the wedding prevented her from speaking her mind.

And from seeing more of Colin. By the time everyone drifted toward the waiting sleighs, he had departed. She probably wouldn't see him for another week.

Heart lightened from the mere glimpse of him, Meg tucked herself into the sleigh. Father stepped in beside her, and they set out across the snowy landscape. Craning her neck, Meg observed her school. Snow piled on its roof gave it the appearance of an iced cake. Above it, branches of the oak sagged with their fluffy, white burden, and in their midst someone perched, knocking the snow away.

"Why is he doing that?" Meg cried.

Father pulled up the horse. "What?"

Meg gestured to the tree and Colin relieving the branches of their excess weight. "He's going to hurt himself."

"Not if he's careful. It's a sturdy tree." Father nodded. "Thoughtful of him. Those branches could go through that roof if they got too heavy and broke off. He's a nice young man."

"Yes." Meg craned her neck around so she could watch him as Father snapped the reins and got the horse going again.

"I'm sorry I can't allow you to associate with him." Father spoke after a few minutes. "If circumstances were different. . ." He sighed. "But they're not. You need a man of substance and property."

Meg caught her breath. "Are you saying you would approve of him if he had property, even though he's a glassblower?"

"It's beside the point, Margaret. He doesn't and never will. Now, what's for dinner?"

"We're having a roast chicken."

"That's good. Very good."

The chicken would be good. The afternoon would not. She must spend it with Joseph, but she could bear it. Father's words lit a spark of hope in her heart, and she determined to nurture it to a flame.

The spark gave her the strength to muster warmth as she served dinner. She needed to say nothing when the men talked of business, but she brought up her plans for a Christmas party at the school during a lull in the discussion.

"Isn't that a great deal of work for you, my dear?" Joseph asked. "Don't you and your father have a party on Christmas Eve, too?"

"Yes, but with Sarah gone, I need something to do, and why delay starting the school until after the first of the year? It's ready now."

Joseph turned to Father. "And you haven't been able to talk her out of this. . .notion of teaching the charcoal burners' and farm laborers' children?"

"It's harmless." Father shrugged. "And working on it makes her happy."

"But those children are such ruffians." Joseph's eyes held concern.

"I want to include all local children eventually. Most of them are well-behaved. The five boys from the charcoal burners are a bit high-spirited," Meg admitted. "But I've managed to get them in line the two times I've encountered them."

"You encountered them twice?" Father and Joseph both frowned at her.

"I knew about the kittens," Father said. "When was the second time?"

"The day I went fishing with—" She pressed her serviette

to her lips and sprang off her chair. "We have a spiced cake for dessert. I'll go make coffee."

She escaped from the dining room before they could question her further.

Meg stood at the window while the coffee brewed, and she watched some gray green finches pecking at grain scattered across the snow. Clustered in the stable doorway, five cats stared at the birds but didn't venture into the cold wetness even for a bit of a hunt.

"Five cats." Meg counted the kittens again. "Wanderer is missing."

She wanted to escape out the back door and hunt the little creature down. His size must make traveling in the snow difficult. Surely he merely slept or hunted inside the stable and wasn't so foolish that he thought he could climb white mountains for adventure. She needed to persuade Father to let her have the wee beastie in the house for his own sake.

In her head she heard Colin calling the kitten a wee beastie, and her heart fluttered. A man who showed such tenderness to a tiny creature deserved to have someone who could love him without reservation. She wanted to. Oh how she wanted to! But her father wouldn't approve, and the man she was supposed to marry waited for her.

Colin and the missing kitten still on her mind, Meg took her tray of coffee and cake into the dining room and discovered her father no longer sat at his place.

"Your father wanted to look over some contracts before he posts them back to Philadelphia tomorrow," Joseph explained. "He thought we would be comfortable here, since the fire is already bright and the room warm."

"Then I'll take coffee in to him." Before Joseph could object, Meg snatched up a plate, fork, and coffee cup.

She intended to ask Father if she and Joseph could look for the kitten. Tramping through the snow, calling for a cat did not give rise to personal conversation. But Father merely nodded in acknowledgment of the refreshment and kept reading. Meg waited a moment, hoping he would understand she wanted his attention. It failed to materialize, so she trudged back to the dining room.

Joseph greeted her with one of his thin-lipped smiles. "Do sit down. We can talk for a while."

"I'd like to go look for my cat." Meg bunched her ruffled white apron between her fingers. "He may be in the stable, but he's not with the other cats, and I don't want him in the snow when night falls."

Joseph stared at her. "You want to tramp about in the snow looking for a useless creature like a cat?"

"Cats are not useless. They keep vermin away from the grain."

"Not if you make pets of them."

"I like animals. They're fun to watch and nice to pet."

"I do not believe in pets." Joseph set the pot down with a *thud*. "Dogs are for herding and guarding, and cats are for killing mice. Horses are for pulling or riding. One does not pamper them or worry about them. Especially with a cat. If it dies, ten more are available to take its place."

Now Meg stared, her mouth open on a gasp. "Surely you don't mean that. We are to care for all God's creatures. They are precious to Him and should be to us."

"Oh, that." Joseph waved his hand in the air as though erasing a slate. "Animals, like some men, are here to serve the rest of us."

"No." Meg took a step backward. "We are the ones who serve. We serve God and His creatures and our fellow man. The more fortunate we are, the more responsibility we have."

"Of course." Joseph smiled, his eyes flat and cool. "We have a responsibility to be good stewards of what we're given and be generous when possible."

"But what of ourselves?" Feeling a little weak in the knees, Meg dropped onto the nearest chair. "We are supposed to give of our abilities to do the Lord's work. I have some skill with teaching; I learned in school with the younger girls, so I want to teach children close to their homes."

"Not after we're married."

"As long as I'm able."

"You won't be able. You won't have time." He drew his chair closer to her, his knees mere inches from hers. "You'll be too busy setting up our home and entertaining."

"Of course I'll do those things for my husband," Meg said, choosing her words with care, "but I will still teach and knit and take food to the sick."

"Not as my wife. I won't have you associating with those people and risk becoming ill."

"But what about church activities? What about serving the Lord?"

"Arranging fetes and so forth, of course." He leaned forward and patted her hand. "That's completely appropriate. And you may embroider handkerchiefs but not knit. Knitting is common."

"I can embroider handkerchiefs?" Meg nearly choked on the words. "When a child is cold, what good is an embroidered handkerchief? How does that demonstrate God's love?"

Joseph shrugged and reached for the coffee. "You take cream and sugar, don't you?"

"I've worked hard to prepare this school," Meg plunged on. "I'm not going to give the children a taste of education then pull it away, while I live in luxury."

"Come, come, you make too much of it." He slid a cup of coffee toward her. "It's not as though these children expect to go to school or even will if it's offered."

Meg held her breath. She counted to ten. When she didn't feel as though she would strangle if she spoke to him, she leaned forward, her hands folded on her knees. "Joseph—"

A knock on the kitchen door interrupted her. She sprang to her feet and sped from Joseph to whoever called at the kitchen on a Sunday afternoon.

"I found the wee beastie outside the glassworks." Colin greeted her with a sodden mass of black-and-white fur limp on his palms. "He'd been chasing the birds that far, I'm thinking."

"Thank you." Her heart soared like a winged creature the cat might chase. "Is he all right?"

"Aye, that he is." Colin smiled. "Now that he's with you."

His eyes held hers, conveying the message he referred to more than the kitten's being all right in her presence. She grinned in return, feeling the same about him, and held out her hands to accept the bedraggled burden.

"I'll make him a box here by the fire. Maybe you would—"

"Good of you to return the cat," Joseph pronounced. "Allow me to recompense you for your time."

A flash shot through Meg's side vision. A silver coin sailed toward Colin's still outstretched hand. An instant before it should have landed in his palm, he shoved his hands into the pockets of his coat, allowing the money to hit the floor with a resounding *ping*.

"I did not bring the cat home for money," Colin said in a voice icier than the snow behind him. "I did it as a favor to Miss Jordan. Now I'll be on my way. 'Tis her wish, you ken."

For your sake, she wanted to cry out.

"Take care of yourself." She hugged the kitten to her. "I'm going to keep this beastie near me all the time now for his own good."

"Thank you." Smiling, Colin tipped his hat to her then spun on his heel and strode off through the packed snow.

"Revolting." Joseph reached past her and slammed the kitchen door. "You lower yourself, Margaret."

"Because I'm going to care for a kitten?"

"Because you care for a mere glassblower. When we're married, you will never associate with the glassblowers or their families."

Meg turned on him. "I will associate with whomever I please. I want to be with glassblowers or anyone else. I'm sure it's what God wants for me."

"Not possible." Joseph curled his upper lip. "You are gently bred and beautiful. You deserve better associates than that."

"I don't deserve anything. I've been blessed is all." She carried the kitten to the arc of warmth around the stove but kept her gaze on Joseph. "Since you think to associate with only those you consider worthy of notice, what is your notion of serving the Lord?"

"I go to church on Sundays and holidays and give generously." He cut himself a slice of the cake still sitting on the worktable and bit off a generous hunk, chewed, and swallowed, while Meg waited for him to say more. "Other than that, I'm far too occupied with my properties to do anything."

"I see." Meg's spine stiffened. "And you're saying that you won't allow your wife to do much more than work on the church fetes?"

"You won't have time."

"Even if I want to use my time for something other than housekeeping and entertaining important people?"

"You won't have a choice."

"I see." Meg took a deep, shaky breath. The kitten's claws dug into her shoulder like a pricking conscience. "Joseph, I need to go to my room. Please excuse me."

Without waiting for him to respond, she strode past him, through the dining room, and up the steps to her bedchamber. Once there she tucked the kitten into a quilt on the floor, then she fell to her knees.

"Lord, I don't want to marry him. I simply can't do it. Surely You don't want this for me either."

She so disliked the idea of marriage to Joseph that she couldn't believe God wanted the union. Yet she couldn't figure out how to make things change. Her father's future depended on the marriage. Colin's future depended on the marriage. His family's future depended on the marriage. As for her future...

"God, I can't do this. I believe You want me to serve You with the school, yet I'm being forced to marry a man who doesn't serve You at all. It's wrong. I can't—I can't—"

She sobbed and didn't care who heard her.

"I thought if I did enough, You would honor that and give me what I want. Is that too much, Lord?" She pounded her fist against her mattress. "I want to teach at the school. I want to bring home kittens or orphans or whoever needs help. I want—"

Her own words began to ring in her ears, and she stopped, choking down the next sob.

She was telling God what she wanted to do for Him. Rocking back on her heels in a puddle of crumpled muslin skirts, she scanned through her mind to think of when she had asked God what He wanted her to do. No time came to mind, not a single prayer, even a brief one. All her prayers regarded what she wanted to happen. She told God; she didn't ask Him.

"But I haven't done anything wrong." The minute she made the statement, she knew it was a poor excuse for going her own way.

Going her own way was doing something wrong. Father denied her little, so she asked for the school, knowing she would get it. And the school cost Father money and resources he couldn't afford. She pursued Colin, knowing he found her attractive. And their relationship put him in Joseph's sights, endangering Colin's future at the glassworks. She had no idea what sort of troubles she had caused others with her willful behavior.

"Lord, I need You to show me what You want for me." She gulped. "Even if that means marrying Joseph."

More peaceful, if not entirely settled in her heart and mind, Meg returned downstairs to clear away the dinner dishes. Joseph was nowhere in sight. Neither was Father. She sliced bread and buttered it, then she set it on a plate with pieces of cheese and ham and some apples and left them on the kitchen table for Father's supper. Back in her bedchamber, she decided to push forward with her party for the potential schoolchildren and listed things she needed to accomplish for both that event and the one for neighbors on Christmas Eve. She worked until the candle guttered and her eyelids drooped. She still hadn't heard Father come home, but she crawled into bed to sleep.

Sometime during the night she heard the sleigh *swoosh* into the stable yard, harness jingling, and a few minutes later the back door closed. Father had returned from wherever he had gone. Meg rolled over and fell into a deeper sleep that lasted until Ilse arrived and the aroma of coffee drifted up to Meg's room.

She dressed with haste and ran downstairs for breakfast.

"You look pretty today." Ilse set a mug of coffee before Meg at the kitchen table. "The wedding must have pleased you."

Only Colin's kiss had pleased her about the wedding, but she mustn't think about that, let alone admit it to the older woman.

"I'm excited," Meg said. "I'm going over to the school to see if I can make tables out of the crates so I can have a bit of a party for the children there next Monday."

"Ya, that would be kind of you." Ilse smiled. "My children are looking forward to the school."

"That pleases me. No eggs. Just some toasted bread."

Meg wolfed down her breakfast and hastened into pattens, warm cloak, hat, and gloves. She would have to walk slowly, and a brisk wind warned her she would be chilled by the time she reached the school. But she didn't care. She was working for the Lord now, not herself.

Despite the cumbersome iron rings on the bottom of the pattens, she trotted along the road, following the ruts of sleigh runners and heavy wagons. Her heart twisted a bit as she passed the glassworks with its twin curls of smoke spiraling into the gray white sky. She employed all her willpower not to stop and pull the bell for admission. She couldn't see Colin again unless something changed.

"It can, Lord. I know it can with Your help."

Though she had no idea how.

She reached the crossroad, where chunks of ice flowed in the stream. A glance at the lightning-struck tree assured her no kitten clung to the branches. Only another hundred yards to her school.

She rounded the corner and stopped, her heart freezing in her chest.

Yesterday an aging oak spread its snow-laden branches over the roof of the school. Today that same tree lay with its branches inside the roof of the school.

Half the roof and one wall were completely destroyed.

fourteen

The goldfinch perfume bottle lay in fragments atop Colin's workbench. He found it the moment he walked into the glassworks on Monday. Considering he left it in the lehr to cool Saturday evening, the ornament could not have broken on its own.

"Aye, and I suspect I ken who 'twas." He let his gaze travel the length of the glasshouse to where Joseph Pyle stood talking with Isaac Jordan.

The men's faces appeared grim. Gray tinged Jordan's complexion, and he stood with his arms crossed over his chest. Pyle leaned forward, making his height advantage over Jordan appear far greater, rather as though he were a bird of prey.

Another image of the man flashed into Colin's mind—Pyle standing behind Meg, his hands clenched, his eyes colder than the snow blanketing the countryside, while he challenged Colin's presence in the kitchen.

The cat had merely been an excuse. Colin could have warmed the creature in his own house and returned it to the stable without disturbing Meg. The need to see her, to receive one of her smiles, to hear her voice flared inside him, and he allowed his feet to carry him to her door.

The sight of her, the hint of apple blossoms mingling with fresh coffee and spices, the brush of her fingers against his added up like treasures, and he stored them in his heart in case she married Pyle.

But she couldn't marry him. Colin understood, empathized with Pyle's wish to marry Meg and have her near him. Colin didn't approve of how Pyle went about compelling her to wed him. At the same time, Jordan had made the debt, had agreed to the bargain. Surely a father who loved his daughter as Jordan loved Meg would never ally her to an unworthy man. Pyle would take care of Meg, cherish her, give her the kind of life Colin could scarcely imagine living, let alone bestow upon a wife. He had to convince himself she was better off with Joseph Pyle in the end so he could let her go. His conscience demanded it. He couldn't let his family down again. She couldn't see her father suffer.

The broken perfume bottle changed all Colin's careful thinking. A man who deliberately smashed a piece of work lacked kindness. Worse, he possessed a streak of meanness that might not stop with cruelty to a glass ornament.

"What happened?"

Colin startled at Thad's voice close behind him, knocking several shards of the finch bottle onto the floor.

"Somebody smashed it." Colin shoved the other pieces onto the stone to be swept up for cullet later. "I left it in the lehr."

"Who would do something like that?" Thad glanced from the fragments to the head of the room.

"Who can get into the glassworks?" Colin asked.

"Any of us with keys. That's you, me, Weber, and the senior apprentice. And Jordan, of course."

"And who was here first this morning?"

"Jordan and Pyle. But if you're thinking someone snuck in here and broke your piece—" Thad shrugged. "I hate to say it, but anyone could bribe someone to open the glassworks. Weber and I wouldn't do it, but the apprentices might wish a little income."

"Or someone welcome in Jordan's house could take his key," Colin mused aloud.

"Colin?" Thad lowered his voice. "What are you suggesting?"

"I'd say 'tis a warning." Colin picked up his pipe and

called over an assistant. "Just the green glass, Louis."

"You're not working on more goblets today?" Louis asked.

"Nay, nor will I be. I'll be making the medicine bottles."

"Yes, sir." The lad darted off with Colin's pipe to fetch the molten glass.

Thad fixed Colin with a crease set between his brows. "A warning for what?"

"To stay away from Meg—Miss Jordan." Colin slid onto his bench to wait for his pipe.

"No, Jordan would never do something like that. He'd just dismiss you. I warned you about that."

"Aye, so you did. So Jordan did." Colin returned his gaze to the two men by the desk. "But I did not say 'twas a warning from himself."

"Pyle?" Thad snatched up his own pipe. "Why would he be in a position to threaten you over Miss Jordan?"

"I should not say. 'Tis only speculation." Colin turned to take the pipe from the assistant.

A glowing mass of molten glass clung to the end of the metal tube. With the pipe balanced on the grating before the bench, Colin inhaled deeply through his nose, set the end of the instrument to his lips, and began to blow in a slow, steady stream of air. A bubble formed in the glass. Colin turned his pipe. The glass shifted, began to form. All that mattered was the glass, the object he created, his work.

The glass would free him from the guilt of abandoning his family. It gave him the means to change their lives. He must not dwell on the pain of giving up Meg for the glass. Surely God would honor his sacrifice.

The glass began to cool, began to turn viscous. Colin removed his tongs from the set of tools at his side and commenced manipulating the caramelized silica into the flat, wide shape of a bottle to hold laudanum to ease pain or an elixir to soothe a sore throat.

The glassworks receded into a background hum of voices, hiss of fire, chink of cooled glass, the music of his life. Peace flowed through him like air through his pipe. All that mattered was the glass, the nearly completed bottle. Part of his mind knew he heard the gate bell ring. On the far side of the furnace from the door, he felt no draft if someone opened it. He focused on the forming mass of green before him, the tongs in his hand, the twist of his wrist—

The door flew open. "Father!" Meg charged into the glassworks, hair tumbling down her back, hat askew. "Father, the school is destroyed!"

Colin dropped his pipe and the nearly finished medicine bottle. The metal pipe hit the grate then the floor with a resounding clang and clatter like a bell losing its clapper. The eyes of the three people in the front of the factory swung his way. No one moved. No one spoke. Leaving the pipe and useless lump of green glass, Colin slid off his bench and stalked to the front of the glassworks.

"What happened?" he asked.

Pyle took a step toward him. "This is none of your concern. Get back to work."

"But 'tis my concern, sir." Colin bowed his head. "I was at the school yesterday after church, and all was well."

"I saw you." Meg still breathed too quickly, and color flamed along her cheekbones. "You were removing snow from the tree branches. But it didn't do any good. The tree has fallen into the building."

"Impossible," Jordan snapped. "That's a sturdy tree."

"It's a very old tree." Pyle yawned behind his rather red hand. "Apparently having a hulking brute like you in its branches wore it out." He snorted as though amused by his insulting words.

"'Tis possible." Colin remained calm on the outside, while his innards roiled. "But unlikely."

"I'd say it's unlikely." Jordan rubbed his temples. "The wind was blowing last night, but not that strongly."

"What does it matter how it happened?" Tears spilled down Meg's cheeks.

Colin clasped his hands behind his back to stop himself from pulling her head against his shoulder.

"I don't have my school now," she sobbed.

"Such a shame," Pyle murmured. "After all that work." He took her hand and tucked it into the crook of his arm. "Come along, m'dear. I'll walk you home and let Mrs. Weber spoil you." He started to pull a glove from his coat pocket, then he tucked it back again.

"I don't want to be spoiled. I want my school." Meg wiped her gloved fingers over her cheeks. "Please, Father, what can be done?"

"I don't know." A muscle twitched at the corner of Jordan's jaw. "I don't know." He cleared his throat. "I'll have to—uh—assess the damage. Joseph, do take her home. Grassick, you have an order to fill."

"Aye, sir." Colin waited until Meg and Pyle left the glassworks before returning his attention to Jordan. "Sir, I'll work through the dinnertime if you'll allow me to do that assessing for you."

"Hmm, well, you may need to come back after supper, too."

"Aye, sir, I'll get that order fulfilled on time." *And remake the goldfinch bottle, though not for its original purpose, the Lord willing.* "Every night, sir, I'll work late if necessary."

"All right then, go." Jordan swept an arm toward the door then pivoted on his heel and shuffled to the desk like a man twenty years his senior.

Colin pulled his coat and hat from hooks by the door, donned them, then set out across the hard-packed snow in the yard. Ice had formed in the ruts from wagon wheels and sleigh runners, so he kept to the deeper snow. The countryside lay in silence save for his footfalls crunching and an occasional branch cracking beneath its burden of white. When he reached the crossroad, he thought he heard children's laughter. Children who wouldn't have their school now, thanks to—

He stopped himself from drawing a conclusion without proof. Just because he didn't like a man, just because that man used his money and influence to gain the lady Colin loved didn't grant him license to make unfounded accusations against him.

"If I found the proof, Lord, I could change Meg's mind."

He rounded the corner and saw the school, half crushed like a child's kicked-in sand castle.

Feeling as though the tree had landed on him, Colin made his inspection then returned the way he had come. He didn't stop at the glassworks. He continued down the road to the Jordans' lane. Around the back he encountered Ilse Weber collecting logs.

"I'll get those for you." Colin relieved her of the burden.

Ilse opened the kitchen door to warmth and the smell of baking apples. "*Danke*, Colin, but you should be working."

"Aye, but I need to speak to Miss Jordan first." He set the logs in the wood box by the stove and smiled at her. "Please."

"Ah, you, you flirt with those eyes, and I'm a married woman."

"No such thing. I'm begging like a stray cur. 'Tis verra important I speak with Miss Jordan."

"I sent her to her room with a cup of chamomile tea. She's upset, she is."

"Please fetch her. She's going to be more—" Colin broke off at the sound of light footfalls on the steps.

A moment later Meg pushed through the kitchen door. "Colin, what are you doing here?"

"I've come to see you, Meg." Ignoring Ilse's gasp, he closed the distance between him and Meg and took both of her hands in his. "You cannot marry Joseph Pyle."

"I beg your pardon?" Her hands writhed in his, but she made no move to pull away. "How can you say something so outrageous? Of course I can marry him. I have no choice but to marry him."

"Aye, that you do. Furthermore, you must make the choice not to marry him."

"And be responsible for you losing your position and your family suffering?" She drew her hands away now and clasped them on her elbows. "The destruction of the school is God's way of telling me I was wrong to think that's what He wanted me to do—teach, that is. I'm supposed to marry Joseph as my father wishes. Now, please leave."

"Please hear me out." Colin kept his hands outstretched in a supplicant's pose. "Meg—"

"She said to leave, Colin." Ilse glided up beside him and laid a gentle hand on his arm. "For your own sake if nothing else, you must get back to the glassworks."

"Aye, I must." Colin met and held Meg's gaze. "But let me have my say, first. Please."

Meg sighed. "All right. Speak, then be gone."

"Thank you." Although for most of his life, he'd spoken nothing but English, except on his brief journeys home, his thoughts suddenly began to form in Gaelic. He struggled to unscramble the languages and spoke with care. "I cannot believe that 'tis God's will for you to marry Joseph Pyle when I have reason to believe the destruction of your school was nay accident and he is responsible."

fifteen

Meg felt as though someone pulled the kitchen floor out from beneath her feet. In a moment she would land in the root cellar or wake from a nightmare. Air refused to reach her lungs, and she swayed.

Colin caught hold of her shoulders and held her steady. "You're all right, lass. I'm here. Nay harm will come to you."

"No." She gave her head a violent shake. "You can't be right. I prayed last night—" She squeezed her eyes shut. "Last night I told Joseph to go away, then I prayed for God to show me what He wanted. I always do what I want, I'm so selfish, and—"

"You're the last person who anyone would call selfish." His fingertips brushed across her cheek, and she realized she was crying.

"Ya," Ilse said, "she's kindness itself."

"No, no." Meg made herself open her eyes and look into Colin's. "Listen to me. Last night I prayed for God to show me what He wants for me. Joseph said I couldn't keep the school, and I came close to saying I wouldn't marry him because he won't allow me to have my kittens or my school or my knitting." She spoke fast to get all the words out. "I prayed for God to show me what He wants and—and the school is destroyed today. Surely this means God wants me to marry Joseph and save you and Father and everything else and serve the Lord as Joseph's wife."

"Not if the tree was destroyed on purpose." Colin's hold on her shoulders tightened. "Meg, it was cut with an ax. I ken the marks. No snow or wind blew that tree over."

"Then God used some mischief maker." Meg stepped

138

away from him and turned her face toward the windows so she could think clearly. "Joseph wouldn't be so cruel."

"Someone made me burn my hand." Colin's voice grew soft. "Joseph Pyle was near the glassworks at the time. Someone smashed a piece of work I was making for you. Joseph Pyle—"

"No, you mustn't say these things about him. He's going to be your master soon."

"And the tree—"

"You need to leave." Meg stepped around him, heading for the door.

"Ya, Colin, you'd best be gone," Ilse added.

"Nay, I will not leave until you hear me out, Margaret Jordan." He followed her to the door and laid his hand against her cheek, gently turning her face toward his. "Please, for your sake. I found a glove in the schoolyard. Did you notice he wasn't wearing gloves today in spite of the cold? His hands were red from it, but only one glove stuck out of his coat pocket."

The scene in the glassworks flashed through her mind, Joseph taking her hand to place on his arm. Then she remembered Joseph bowing over her hand when he left her at the house. No gloves. Red hands. A supple leather mitt protruding from one coat pocket.

"But what—what does this mean?" she whispered. "Colin?"

She held out her hands, needing something solid to cling to, as her world that seemed so certain—unhappy but certain—an hour ago crumbled beneath her. Colin took her hands then released them and wrapped his arms around her. She buried her face in the rough wool of his coat, inhaling his scent of wood smoke and the freshness of the winter day.

He crooned to her, words that weren't English yet comforting in their sibilant melody. "God has a plan for you, lass," he said, switching to English. "I can't accept He will use a deliberately cut tree to reveal it to you."

"But—"

"Miss Meg," Ilse broke in. "Your father—"

The back door sprang open. Meg jumped away from Colin, her face flaming. "Father, I—"

"What are you doing here, Grassick?" Father's dark amber eyes blazed.

Meg pressed her hand to her lips. "Father, please, don't misunderstand—"

"Hush, lass, I can explain." Colin took her hand in his. "I came to warn your daughter of Joseph Pyle's treachery."

"I beg your pardon?" Father enunciated each word with care. "Ilse, what sort of carrying-on are you allowing behind my back and in my own house? I hold you responsible."

"He was comforting me." Meg tugged on Father's sleeve. "Please, listen to what Colin has to say. It's—distressing."

"What I find distressing," Father said, "is finding my daughter being embraced by one of my employees. Now get yourself back to work, Grassick, or you can go pack your things and leave."

"No," Meg protested.

"Nay, sir." Colin stood his ground, a full head taller than Father and far broader in the shoulders. Solid. Dependable. Noble.

Meg's heart cried out for a life beside this man.

"You may dismiss me if you wish, sir," Colin said, "but my conscience would never stop pricking me if I left to save my own skin and risked Meg's."

"She is Miss Jordan to you, Grassick." Father planted his hands on his hips. "You've been warned once too often."

"Aye, sir." Colin sighed. "And the matter stands. I will not risk her future with a man who destroys property, when it could be people one day."

Meg shivered and wanted the warmth of Colin's arm around her again.

Father scowled. "You make a grave accusation, Grassick. The consequences could be serious."

"Aye, I ken the risk, but the truth speaks for itself." Colin reached past Father and opened the door. "Will you come with me, sir, Miss Jordan? I'll show you the evidence."

Father hesitated, and Meg held her breath. Then Father nodded. "Because I think you're a good man, I'll let you have your say in full. Margaret—"

Meg was already racing to find her cloak and pattens. She joined the men in the stable yard, where Father was harnessing the horses to the sleigh. With three passengers, they sat close together like a family. If only...

Surely God didn't want her married to a man who could be dangerous at the worst and destroyed things important to others in order to get his own way at the least.

The sleigh runners hissed over the snow, and the horses' hooves crunched through the icy crust. The air lay so still, smoke from the glassworks and charcoal burners soared straight into the sky, white columns against the pale blue. Meg clasped her arms across her middle and willed the sleigh to go faster while her stomach churned with the anticipation of seeing her school in ruins.

"All those beautiful windows you made," she murmured.

"The building can be repaired, lass." Colin smiled down at her.

Meg knew she should say she didn't want to restore the building, that she must marry Joseph and be done with the school. It had brought nothing but trouble and expense. She should have known from the day she found the smashed windows she wasn't supposed to carry on her work. Yet her heart ached at the prospect of giving up her school or the cats or her newfound pleasure in knitting. Her insides quaked at the notion of marrying a man who treated others with such disregard and things with respect.

Her lower lip began to hurt, and she realized she held it clamped between her teeth. She made herself stop, but her jaw felt as rigid as the trunk of the oak beside her school. The trunk of the oak that used to stand beside her school.

The sleigh swept around the curve in the road, and the sight of the school sprang into view. Meg covered her eyes, unable to see the caved-in roof, the sagging wall.

"Did you see anything unusual here, Margaret?" Father asked.

"No, sir." Meg gulped. "I saw the tree down and ran back to the glassworks. It's—horrible."

"Aye, hinnie, 'tis a pathetic sight." Colin touched her cheek.

Father glared at him. "You haven't proven anything to us yet."

"I will." Colin sprang from the sleigh and held out a hand to Meg.

She took it and stepped to the snowy ground. They stood, hands still clasped, while Father secured the horses. She avoided Colin's eyes but welcomed the strength of his hand.

"Let's see this proof." Father tramped through the snow, his footfalls sounding like an ax cutting through wood.

As an ax had cut through the tree trunk. Meg stood between Father and Colin and stared at the slashes in the trunk, not all the way through, just enough to weaken the oak.

"I could not clear the higher branches of their snow." Colin spoke in a low voice as though afraid someone would overhear. "They were too thin to hold my weight. But I thought what I did would be enough to protect the building."

"It would have been without this." Father gestured to the split trunk. "Maybe a branch or two would have taken off a couple of shingles but not this destruction."

His face appeared gray in the brilliant light of sun on snow.

"But this is no proof that Joseph did this," Father added. "Anyone wanting to make mischief could have. Think of those broken windows."

"Aye, but who would have wanted to smash windows?" Colin asked. "Have you or your daughter the enemies?"

"No, but Joseph hasn't any cause either."

"He does." Meg felt ill. "I made it clear to him that I thought the school more important than he is. I didn't like him telling me I could only arrange fetes for the church and things like that when I'm his wife. I was willful about it." She swallowed. "Like I'm willful about everything."

"You've been indulged." Father squeezed her shoulder. "But don't blame yourself for this. We don't have proof one way or another."

"Except for that." Colin pointed to something nearly the color of the bark snagged on a knot protruding from the side of the trunk.

Meg leaned forward to get a better look. So soft and supple it molded itself to the tree, the glove hung torn and dirty, a mute testimony to its owner. A match to the glove in Joseph's pocket.

"I'm thinking he doesn't know where he lost it," Colin said. "But he'll come here to look eventually."

"He should have come here first," Meg whispered. "We'd never have known."

"He might have intended to." Father stepped away from the tree. "He wouldn't expect you to come here and find the disaster so early if at all until the snow melts."

"Nor I." Colin faced Father. "Do you believe me, sir? And shall I tell you about the accidents in the glassworks? Nay proof there, you ken, and who else would wish to harm or discredit me?"

"Why would Joseph?" Father returned.

"Because of me." Meg curled her fingers and squeezed for something to hold on to. "Because I insisted on being friendly with Colin and showed my preference for him over Joseph. If I didn't insist on having everything my own way, he might not be pressuring Father over the loan money and—and—"

"Even if that were true, 'tis no excuse for a man's behavior," Colin said.

"And little proof to lay against a man of Joseph's prominence," Father pointed out. "I won't make accusations against him."

Meg stared at Father. "But shouldn't we ask him? That is, are you going to let him get away with this?"

"We don't know he's getting away with anything." Father removed the glove from the tree. "Maybe he was here inspecting the damage, as we are."

"With all due respect, sir," Colin said, "this was here before Mr. Pyle could have gotten here."

"Oh, uh, true."

Now that he held the glove, Meg saw it was sodden, as though melting snow had soaked through the leather. No snow remained on the tree to drip as the sun melted it. None had remained on the tree when they arrived.

"We should at least ask him," she pointed out.

Father turned on his heel and tramped back to the sleigh. Meg gazed after him for a moment then turned to Colin.

He gripped her hand. "We need to persuade your father to talk to Pyle, you ken."

"Yes." Head down, Meg followed her father, drawing Colin with her.

Father stood at the horses' heads, stroking their gray noses and staring at the sky. "If we're wrong," he said as though talking to himself, "he will forget he's given me a two-week grace period and call in the loan now. I can't let him have the glassworks. I've worked too hard for it." He faced Colin. "And you know as soon as he is the owner, he'll dismiss you to get you away from Meg."

"Aye, I ken." Colin's face paled against the vivid red of his hair. "My faith has been lacking in a number of areas in my life, mostly that I haven't trusted the Lord to take care of my family, insisting I do it all myself. But how can I see my family in comfort here in America, giving them the grand futures, when Meg's future as that man's wife looks to be one of misery? I'll risk losing my position here and return to Scotland before I see Meg married to that man."

"Colin, no." Meg clasped his hand between both of hers. "No, you can't do that. I want your family here and you to keep your position."

"Aye, you want." Colin smiled at her. "But is that what the Lord wants? Or are we to trust Him to show us a different plan, one that is different from what we're thinking?"

Meg started to speak, then she clamped her lips together. Colin was right. If Joseph continued to go around causing damage to property when people thwarted his will, he might end up harming a person.

She took a deep breath. "I'll do what you wish, Father."

"And I also, sir."

"It's a risk that could hurt all of us," Father said. "But it's one we have to take."

sixteen

"Is it faith or foolishness?" Father asked the question as he entered the house.

They were the first words he'd spoken since leaving the school. They paused at the glassworks long enough for Colin to return to work then they swept up the lane to the house. While Father took the horses to the stable, Meg ran inside to warm herself by the fire and prepare hot tea. She told Ilse to go home, that she would see to their meals.

Now Father stood wiping snow from his boots, rubbing his hands together, and gazing past Meg as though posing the question to someone other than her.

She chose to answer. "I'm trying to work that out, but I think it's faith. I've been going my own way and not asking which way to go."

"You had a good teacher in me, daughter." Father came forward and hugged her. "I did the same in not asking the Lord if I should open the glassworks. I wanted to do this in memory of my father. I should have kept my promise to your mother. But Joseph offered to lend the money, so I went ahead. We'll be profitable soon. The orders are coming in. But it's not soon enough. Joseph will break his word to extend the contract past Christmas because you won't agree to marry him."

"And there's nothing you can do about it?" Meg clung to him as she had when a small child, seeking comfort from a nightmare or skinned knee. "There's no one else you can borrow from?"

"There is." Father moved to the stove and held his hands to the warmth. "I approached some bankers on my last

146

journey to Philadelphia. They didn't want to take the risk, but I have orders I can show them. Joseph would be a fool to get rid of Grassick, but he will out of spite."

"Because I pursued him."

"I didn't see him running away, daughter." Father gave her a sad smile. "The two of you. . ."

Meg waited. Father remained silent.

She licked her dry lips. "When will we talk to Joseph?"

"Call it the weakness of my belief that the Lord will work this out according to His will," Father said, "but I'd rather wait until I hear from the bankers."

"And if they say no?"

Father squared his shoulders. "We will still talk to Joseph about the incidents. In the meantime, my dear, don't let him press his suit."

Meg squirmed. "He'll suspect something. I can't do this to you or Colin. I'd rather marry Joseph than see the two of you suffer."

"It's not your decision, Margaret."

"But—" She bowed her head. "Yes, sir."

She didn't know how she would obey her father, knowing it risked his future and Colin's.

"Go pack your things," Father said. "I'll go ask the Webers if you can stay with them."

Her proximity to Colin alone would anger Joseph. Nonetheless, Meg ran upstairs and began to pack a small trunk with clothing for several days. In the kitchen again, she filled a basket with some delicacies for the Webers—a loaf of sugar, a tin of chocolate, butter, jam, and a packet of raisins. She thought for a moment then hefted in flour and spices and more dried fruits. They would bake for the Christmas Eve party, and the children could help, stealing as much dough as they liked. It was the least she could do for destroying their chance at an education.

When Father returned to collect her, she was hauling a

sack of flour from the pantry. He raised his eyebrows but said nothing. He took the bag from her and carried it to the waiting sleigh. He returned for her trunk, and she followed him, swinging the basket. In moments Father drew the horses up before the Webers' cottage.

The Webers ran out to greet Meg and her father, Ilse and Hans along with their three children, who ranged in age from six to fourteen. Neat and clean and smiling, the children seized the food and insisted they carry it into the house for Meg.

"Do you enjoy baking, Gretta?" she asked the eldest.

She nodded, her blond braids flopping against her shoulders. "Yes, I always help Momma."

"I don't bake." Hans, the youngest and only boy, wrinkled his nose. "I only eat because I'm going to be a glassblower."

If the glassworks still existed.

Meg determined to make things work out for the sake of these children, too.

"You can eat as much as your momma says you can." Meg resisted the urge to hug him, and she returned to the yard to bid her father farewell. "God be with you and the bankers," she whispered.

He kissed the top of her head and climbed aboard the sleigh. "I'll leave the horses at the inn and take the next stage."

He clucked his tongue and snapped the reins. The horses trotted forward. The sleigh swept around the corner and disappeared.

Meg pressed her folded arms to her belly to minimize the emptiness inside. "Lord, what is the right answer? I want to know now."

No answer came to her, so she returned to the house and plunged into baking preparations. Martha Dalbow joined them later in the day, and the time flew by. As occupied as she was, Meg kept glancing out the windows, hoping for a glimpse of Colin, fearing a sight of Joseph. She saw neither of them. Hans Weber said Colin was working late at the glassworks.

"He will be all the week." Mr. Weber shook his head. "That young man works too hard. He needs a pretty wife to come home to like I do."

Ilse laughed and blushed, and the emptiness inside Meg grew. This kind of love was what she wanted. She saw it in them, in Martha and Thad, in Sarah and Peter. She doubted she would find it with Joseph. His actions, even if he were not guilty of cutting the tree and destroying Colin's work, assured her that her first impression stood solid. What she would say to him upon their next meeting, she didn't know.

Late the following afternoon she needed to find out. He rode up to the Webers' front door shortly after dinner. Meg saw him through the parlor window and grabbed her cloak off a hook in the kitchen before running to answer his knock.

"Don't go anywhere with him," Ilse insisted.

"I won't." Meg opened the door and stepped onto the stoop, shutting herself outside. "How are you, Joseph?"

"I'm well." He eyed her up and down. "You have flour on your hem."

"I wasn't expecting a guest." She shook out her skirt, sending some of the flour onto his shining boots. "May I assist you with something?"

"Why are you here, and where is your father?" He delivered the questions like a volley of gunfire.

"Father is away, so I'm staying here."

"I should have been told."

"Why?"

"I'm your affianced husband."

Meg wrapped her cloak more tightly around her shoulders against the brisk wind. "No, you're not." She made herself look into his eyes. "Nor will you be until we have made the impending marriage official."

"Which is right now. If your father is so irresponsible

he runs off and leaves you in the protection of these people"—he sneered at the simple, whitewashed cottage—"then you need to be allied with my name for the sake of your reputation."

"My reputation?" Meg drew herself up to her full height. "No one in this county is more respectable than Ilse and Hans Weber. My reputation is likely safer with them than with you."

"Indeed." Joseph smiled, and his eyes glowed with such a cold blue light that Meg felt as though he shoved an icicle through her chest. "You don't understand, Margaret. I can destroy your father and that Scot you fancy. If I can't have you as my wife, I will have the glassworks as my business, and all these good people you think so highly of for no good reason will be out of work. They'll be on the roads and so will you."

"No." Meg flattened her hands against the door behind her for support. "I won't let that happen."

"You'll have no choice unless it's to marry me."

"Why?" She cried out in desperation. "Why do you want to marry me so much that you'd destroy others' lives?"

Joseph shrugged. "Because I want what I want. You're the prettiest and most loved girl in the county. The best. I must have the best."

Meg stared at him, wide-eyed. "I'm not the best, Joseph. I'm selfish and self-centered and want—"

She caught her breath. With her words seeming to ring around the yard like the gate bell, she heard them again and again and realized how close to Joseph's words they sounded. *I want. . . I want. . .*

"We can talk again after Father returns." She turned the door handle.

Joseph caught her wrist. "You will not walk away from me until I say you can."

"You have no right to tell me to stay here." She struggled to free herself.

His grip tightened. "When you're my wife or I own the glassworks—"

"Stop it." Meg wrenched her hand free and pounded her fist on the door. "I will never be your wife, and you will never own the glassworks, once Father hears of this."

"You'd prefer your father lose everything for the sake of your delicate sensibilities?" Joseph laughed. "That won't get you very far when you're homeless."

"We won't be homeless once the bank—" Meg slapped her hand across her lips—too late. She'd let the cat out of the bag.

&

Colin nodded to Louis, the senior apprentice who usually helped him. "This is the last of the purple bowls we'll be making for this order if you'd like to go to your supper."

"Not if you're going to stay and work, sir." Louis, young, fair, and eager to please, hovered near Colin's bench. "We still have the purple silica if you'd like to finish that set of goblets. I was counting them, and with the twelve at the Jordan house, you only have three to go."

Colin had made several of Meg's goblets on Monday out of pique that she insisted she was responsible for fixing everything. Other than carrying her off to one of the states he'd heard about, where couples could marry without any sort of notice—rather like Scotland's own Gretna Green—he didn't know how else to stop her, except to pray for the truth to come forth and the situation to resolve. Even if that meant he was wrong and Joseph Pyle was a decent, if somewhat greedy, man, Colin wanted the best for Meg.

Finishing the goblets felt like defeat, as though he had given in—or up. Yet his practical side told him not to let the already-heated purple glass go to waste and have to be reheated at another time.

"All right," he agreed, "we'll finish the goblets."

"Right." Louis took Colin's pipe and dashed off for the vat of molten glass.

Colin pulled the crate of finished goblets off the shelf and set several on top to study their lines. His tongs, pincers, and calipers lay spread out on his workbench. Other than the crackle of the fire in one furnace and the grate of the door as Louis reached in to draw out the hot glass, the factory lay quiet. Lamps lit the interior. Darkness spread across the outside save for the luminescence of the snow.

A shadow moved against the whiteness. Footfalls crunched past the windows. Then the door opened and Joseph Pyle stood in the opening, frigid air swirling around him and through the building.

"You're dismissed, Grassick," he announced.

Colin met Louis's gaze and indicated he should proceed with the glass, before turning back to Pyle. "By whose orders?"

"Mine." Pyle smiled, his eyes cold. "I own this glass-works now."

"Is that so?" Colin reached out one hand for his pipe, molten glass glowing on the end. "I'll be hearing that from Mr. Jordan before I take an order from you."

He set the pipe to his lips and began to blow in a slow, steady stream that belied the turmoil inside him. Pyle couldn't possibly own the glassworks yet. Jordan said he had until Christmas.

"Put that pipe down, and get out of here." Pyle marched forward.

"The door, sir." Louis ran to close it. "The cold air will ruin the glass."

"Quitting will ruin the glass, too." Pyle's smile widened. "Quite unfortunate for Isaac Jordan's former customer."

If he didn't need to maintain an even exhalation, Colin would have laughed.

Pyle turned to Louis. "Get out, boy. I wish to say a few things to Grassick in private."

"But—but—" Louis stammered.

Never taking his eyes from his work, Colin pointed a

pinkie toward the door.

"If you think it's all right." Louis snatched up his coat and cap and fled.

Colin continued to work, turning the pipe, watching the bubble form, the glass shape.

"If you weren't here, Grassick," Joseph growled, "Margaret would be grateful to me for offering her marriage."

Colin picked up his tongs.

"You've turned her head." Pyle advanced, stepping sideways to avoid the hot glass at the end of the pipe. "You, a mere workman."

Colin applied the tongs to pinch the glass for the stem.

Pyle slid behind him, raising the hairs on the back of Colin's neck. "I could make her a governor's wife, and she wants a glassblower."

Contempt dripped from Pyle's tone.

The tone, the words rang like sweet music in Colin's ears. Meg must have said something to Pyle.

"You'll give her nothing but grief," Pyle continued.

Not so. Colin would give her love.

"That is, if you're still here. Which you won't—" Pyle lunged, snatching the pipe from Colin's hand.

The glass flew off the end. Colin ducked, twisted, rolled away from the pipe's hot tip.

"Think she'll like you with your face scarred?" Pyle plunged the pipe toward Colin.

He snatched up one of the finished goblets and threw it. Pyle deflected it with the pipe like a cricket ball and bat, sending the heavy glass soaring toward Colin. He sprang to his feet. The goblet missed and smashed against a workbench.

Colin vaulted the bench and snatched up the crate. Glasses flew, shattering like discordant music.

Another note sounded, high-pitched and shrill. Meg's scream. Colin looked. A mistake. Pyle leaped at him, the pipe swooping toward Colin's face.

"No!" Meg cried.

Colin dove for Pyle's legs. Meg sprang at his back. They struck at the same time. Pyle dropped with a shout, a *thud* and *tinkle* of glass, and *clang* of metal on stone. He lay in a shower of shattered amethyst glass, the hot end of the blowpipe against his cheek.

seventeen

For several seconds, nothing, no one in the glasshouse moved. Even the fire merely hissed as it began to die on its grate. Then Colin shot to his feet, kicked aside shards of glass, its tinkling breaking the stillness, and crouched beside Joseph to pull the pipe free.

"Is he—gone?" Meg whispered.

It sounded like a shout to her ears.

"Stunned is all." Colin touched the blowpipe. "And he'll have a frightful scar."

"He intended you to have one." Meg staggered to her feet and closed the distance between her and Colin. She wanted to touch him, hold on to his solidity and strength, but she kept her hands pressed to her sides. "He was swinging it at your face."

"Aye, he thought you would not care for me if I had the scar on my face." Colin set the pipe on his workbench then slipped his arms around Joseph and rose, all without looking at Meg. "If you'll be kind enough to get the door for me, I'll carry him to my cottage. Perhaps Hans could be fetching the apothecary."

"Of course."

Before Meg or Colin reached the door, it flew open and Louis, Thad, and Hans rushed in. They halted at the sight of Colin's burden.

"What happened?" Mr. Weber asked.

"He had a wee bit of an accident." Colin shifted Joseph to drape him over his shoulder. "Louis, be a good lad and fetch an apothecary or whatever you have here."

"Yes, sir." Louis bolted out the door.

"He said Pyle was talking ugly," Thad explained, "so he came to fetch us. We're sorry we didn't get here sooner. Are you or Miss Margaret injured?"

"I'm all right," Meg said.

Except for her spirit, which ached like a wound.

"I am, too." Colin headed out the door, paused on the threshold long enough to face Meg. "I'll be calling on you later, if I may."

"Of course." Her response was automatic not warm.

A light flared in Colin's eyes then dimmed. Without another word he spun on his heel and vanished into the night.

Thad slipped his arm around Meg. "Let's get you back to the Webers'. Ilse and Martha will likely have gallons of coffee brewing and piles of sandwiches waiting."

"I'm sure Colin will be hungry." Meg felt too numb to be hungry, though a hot drink sounded good.

Thad led her away. Hans stayed in the glassworks to close up the furnace and extinguish the lamps. The broken glass would be swept up and melted down to make something else. What, Meg neither knew nor cared. It wouldn't be goblets for her new home. The notion should elate her. Joseph had shown his true nature, and no one would expect her to marry him.

Not that anyone would want to marry her, she realized, now that she knew her own true nature.

They reached the Webers' cottage. Thad took her cloak. Ilse nudged her into a kitchen chair and curled Meg's hands around a mug of hot coffee with instructions to drink. Meg felt like a marionette with several people pulling her strings.

"We all want to know what happened," Ilse said. "Thad, go see what's afoot. Where did they all go?"

"Colin's." Thad opened the door. "I'll send Martha over and head to Colin's."

"I should go do something to help." Meg started to rise.

Ilse held her in place with a hand on her shoulder. "You

stay there and warm yourself."

"I'm not cold." Yet as she took a sip of coffee, Meg realized she was.

Ilse draped a quilt over Meg's shoulders. "There now, you've had a terrible shock. We all thought Mr. Pyle was such a good man."

"He always wanted his own way." Meg's hands shook, and she set her cup down. "He picked out things he wanted and did anything necessary to get them. I was one of those things—like fine windows and furnishings for his house. And Colin—" She put her head on her folded arms atop the table. "I nearly killed Colin."

"*Nein. Nein.*" Ilse knelt and wrapped her arms around Meg. "You did no such thing. Now then, would you like to go to your bed?"

"I'd rather wait."

Colin arrived within the hour, along with Hans and Thad.

"The sheriff took Pyle to Salem City," Thad announced.

Meg dropped the knife with which she was cutting slices of cake. "The sheriff took him?"

"Aye, Louis is a quick-thinking lad." Colin retrieved the knife from the table and slid it into her hand. "He sent the apothecary here then went on to collect the sheriff."

"And Pyle was arrested?" Ilse shook her head. "I never thought I'd see it."

"Is he well enough to go to jail?" Meg gazed up at Colin, so close to her yet too far away.

"He'll do." He tucked a curl behind her ear. "He's got a headache and a nasty burn, but he's awake and blaming—well, he's a frightened man."

"You can say it, Colin." Meg gripped the edge of the table. "He's blaming me. It's all my fault, and I'm no better than he is."

A chorus of protests rose.

Colin tilted her chin up with a forefinger and looked into

her eyes. "What makes you say something like that, hinnie?"

"He would stop at nothing to get his own way. I insist on mine, too." Meg licked her dry lips. "I claimed I was doing the Lord's work, but I was doing mine. Is that so different than Joseph wanting the best of everything to glorify himself?"

"You were not trying to bring glory to yourself. How could you ever think so?"

A murmur of agreement ran around the kitchen.

"Isn't going my own way, saying that I want to do this and I want to do that bringing glory to myself?" Meg hugged her middle. "I never once asked God if I was doing what He wanted. I asked my earthly father, who always gives me what I want, except for freedom from Joseph, and I've brought harm through my willfulness. I was so determined I wouldn't marry Joseph that I told him too much and he went straight to the glassworks to attack you."

Colin gave her a gentle smile. "Nay harm's been done. We're all right."

"Are we?" Meg flung out her arms and stalked across the kitchen so she could face everyone. "Joseph may be in jail, but my father still owes him money. He will still own the glassworks, and Colin can still lose his position if Father can't get the loan he needs. You could all lose your positions. You've witnessed Joseph at his worst, and he apparently harms those who thwart him."

"Which is why you cannot wed him," Colin said.

"No, I cannot, and although I want to marry you so much, I can't ever hope to do so."

⁂

Colin set down his pipe and rubbed his eyes. He felt as though the sand that went into making the silica had been poured into his sockets. He needed rest. Yet sleep eluded him and had in the three nights since Joseph Pyle tried to attack him with a hot blowpipe.

Pyle was out of the jail, though facing charges of assault.

He claimed he was defending himself, but even if people doubted the word of a mere glassblower, no one questioned Meg's integrity in her account of the incident.

The other incidents, the hot grate on the workbench, the broken bottle, and the hacked tree, Pyle denied and no one could prove. Since he lay at home, suffering a septic wound from his assault on Colin, he would likely have to pay a fine and nothing more. That left him free to do as he pleased with the glassworks if Jordan didn't obtain the loan money by other means, since Pyle no longer wished to marry Meg for payment. Despite her freedom from that burden, Meg refused to let Colin court her.

"My wanting to be with you has caused nothing but trouble," she insisted.

"But surely You don't want us apart now, Lord," Colin cried aloud to the empty factory.

And why not?

That question sent him pacing the aisles of the glassworks between workbenches and molds, furnaces and lehrs, until he came to rest at one of the windows, his brow against the cold glass.

He'd come to America to help his family. Or so he had told himself. Now he began to wonder if he acted no differently than Meg—going his own way because it was something he wanted, yet excusing the behavior with the claim it was what God wanted.

"But I'm here now, Lord, and my family is thousands of miles away. Meg may as well be. I don't know what to do."

Which might be the best place in the world to be—so uncertain he had no choice but to let the Lord take over.

"But my family—" He stopped, recalling a verse his mother often quoted.

"Wherefore, if God so clothe the grass of the field, which to day is, and to morrow is cast into the oven, shall he not much more clothe you, O ye of little faith? . . . Take therefore no thought for the morrow: for the morrow shall take thought for the things of itself."

She was a great one for having the faith through difficult times. If she, a widow with five children to care for, believed the Lord would show them a way to get through life, then Colin could do the same. Or at the least, he could try. He would trust that the Lord would see to the future and keep working as long as he was allowed to do so. He knew exactly where to start.

Fatigue slipping from his shoulders, Colin returned to his workbench and picked up the drawing he'd made of the goldfinch.

❧

Candles blazed in every room of the Jordan house, and fires blazed on the hearths, staving off the cold sweeping through the rooms each time the front door opened to admit another group of people. Thus far on this Christmas Eve, friends and neighbors braved another snowstorm to partake of the Jordans' Christmas Eve party. People Meg loved to see were laughing and chattering and consuming mounds of food and bowls of hot, spiced cider. She especially enjoyed watching Peter and Sarah together. They glowed whenever they caught each other's gaze. Meg's heart leaped with joy for her dearest friend's happiness.

She jumped with anticipation and apprehension every time the door swung in; Gretta rushed up to take hats and cloaks, and Ilse collected contributions of sweets and savories. She anticipated Father's arrival, hoping, praying for good news, fearing the answer because she wanted it so much.

She wanted Colin to walk through the door, too. But she'd given him up, and only the Lord could give him back if He wished.

Knowing this didn't stop her from jumping and staring toward the kitchen every time she moved near enough to hear the back door open.

"Mar–ga–ret." Sarah drew the name out close to Meg's ear. "I've been talking to you for five minutes, and you keep staring at that door."

"I'm sorry." Meg rubbed her hot cheeks. "I thought I heard someone arrive through the back door."

"How can you hear anything above this din?" Sarah slipped her arm through the crook of Meg's elbow. "Let's steal five minutes in your room. No one will miss us, and I simply must know what happened with Joseph. How could we have all been so wrong?"

"We were deceived by his good looks and wealth."

"You weren't deceived." Sarah hugged Meg. "I owe you an apology."

"You had my future security in your heart, as Father did. So no apology—oh!"

"Isaac, you're home!" someone cried from the parlor.

"Father." Meg whirled on her heel, sending the lace flounces on her gown swirling around her like snow. "You got home in time." She dashed through the crowd of guests and flung herself into his outstretched arms.

Snow covered his coat, and he smelled of leather, wet wool, and pipe smoke. Dark circles rimmed his eyes, but the dark amber irises glowed as though candles burned behind them.

"You look lovely, daughter." He held her at arm's length.

Around them guests stood back and grinned at the reunion.

"I didn't think you'd get here and feared I'd be spending Christmas alone."

"I wouldn't make you do that if I had to swim across the bay to get here." He hugged her again then released her. "If my study isn't full of people, may we have a few minutes there?"

"Shed that wet coat first," Meg said, "and I'll shoo anyone out."

By the time she'd displaced a handful of gentlemen complaining about how President Madison's policies would ruin them all then collected a hot drink and plate of food,

Father had changed his clothes and joined her in his study. Not until the door closed, blocking out the gaiety of the guests and clatter of crockery, did Meg realize what news he might bring. Her stomach began to ache, and she sank onto the edge of a chair.

"What—happened in Philadelphia?"

"First things first." Father began to munch on a slice of ham rolled around a hunk of cheese and spread with mustard. "Tell me what happened here. I've heard some of it, but I want to know everything."

Meg told him. "It was all my fault. I slipped and told Joseph what you were doing in Philadelphia."

"He was bound to find out anyway." Father selected a dried cherry tart and took a healthy bite. "They don't have food like this in the city."

"But, Father." Meg slid farther forward in her chair. "I told him, and he attacked Colin. Or tried to."

"He failed."

"But he won't next time. Next time he'll dismiss him, and that could be worse than a scar. I can't marry Joseph now, even if he still wanted to marry me—which he doesn't—but I've decided I can't associate with Colin either."

"The poor lad. Why would you break his heart like this? Don't you care for him after all?"

"I do." Meg gulped. "More than anything. But I caused so much trouble setting my cap for him it can't be right."

"Seems to me Joseph caused the trouble, not you, my dear."

"Well yes, but if I hadn't been so willful, wanting everything my own way—"

"We don't know what would have happened instead." Father gave her a gentle smile. "One thing I did while waiting about in the city was talk to an old friend from Princeton. He's a man of deep faith, but I've never asked him about it until now." He leaned forward. "I see now that we've been going our own way and not trusting the Lord to either guide us or help us. We are doing good, we say, so we think it's right."

Meg nodded.

"And that makes us worry when things don't go our own way."

She nodded harder.

"But good doesn't mean right." Father rose and rounded the desk. "I got a no the first time I tried a city banker, so I took Joseph's terms, thinking I was doing good for you. But after the incident with the tree, I knew I had to try again, humble myself if necessary. But first I prayed and left it in the Lord's hands. It may be the first time in my life I've done that."

"I prayed, and the next day the school caved in."

"Destroyed by someone's hand. Don't you understand?" Father moved to crouch before her and took her hands in his. "God allowed this so I would see Joseph for the greedy, selfish, and dangerous man he is, not so you would think you should marry him."

Tension inside Meg eased just a bit. She still had to ask, "What about the glassworks? Everyone's positions there?"

"Safe." Father broke into the biggest grin she'd ever seen on his face. "When I asked for a loan before, I didn't have the orders I do now. With these new contracts for glass, we'll make a profit in no time and pay off my debt to Joseph. In fact, I paid him before I came home. He can't threaten any of us any longer."

She covered up the stab of disappointment that she couldn't celebrate this moment with Colin and grinned back. "Then let us join our friends and give thanks to God for the birth of His Son."

"Let's. I believe I just heard some people arrive." Father rose, a little stiffly, and drew Meg with him.

They exited the study. Indeed several more people were crowding through the front door: Sarah's parents and brothers, and behind them, a parcel in his hands, his bright hair dusted with snow, was Colin.

Meg pressed her hand to her lips to stop herself from calling his name. She didn't know why he'd come. Father began to introduce him to everyone, his voice ringing out with pride.

"This is my master glassblower, Colin Grassick, come all the way from Edinburgh, Scotland, to bless us with his presence."

Colin smiled to the ladies, who preened before his charm, and shook hands with the men, who appeared a bit surprised. No one snubbed him. They wouldn't. He had been presented as Father's guest.

Across the entry hall, Meg caught Sarah's questioning glance and shrugged. She didn't know what was afoot. She ached for Colin to speak to her, wish her a blessed Christmas if nothing else. Hearing his voice, seeing his smile, even past the heads of two dozen people, smoothed balm on her bruised spirit.

Then only a dozen people stood between them. Half a dozen melted away. Three. Two. . .

He stood in front of her, holding out his parcel. "A wee gift for you, hinnie."

"Th–thank you." Aware that the crowd watched her, Meg took the package and looked at him. "Should I open it?"

"Of course," people chorused.

"Aye, open it." Colin smiled. "'Twas to be a wedding gift and perhaps still is."

"No no. I don't have to marry Joseph now. That is—" Her hands shook.

"Aye, I ken. Your father stopped to talk to me on his way home." He took back the parcel. "I'll be holding it."

"Thank you." Fingers clumsy, Meg untied the string and allowed the brown paper wrapping to fall back. Meg thought she gasped, but she couldn't be sure amid the collective inhalation.

Before her, nestled in a bed of tissue paper, rested a

goldfinch as delicate and detailed as the ones who populated the countryside, brownish in the winter but golden in summer.

" 'Tis a perfume bottle in which to store your apple blossom scent."

"Colin, I—" Tears blurred the work of art before her, and her throat closed.

"Martha Dalbow says the goldfinch takes a partner for all his life," Colin said, his rich voice flowing around her like music.

"If he sings as well as he talks," the pastor said from the parlor doorway, "we have to get him into the choir."

Meg choked on a giggle.

"So what better gift for a bride than a goldfinch?" Colin continued as though no one had spoken.

"But I'm not going to be a bride," Meg murmured. "You know that."

"I ken nay such thing." He tucked one hand beneath her chin and tilted her face up. "I cannot offer you many fine servants and a grand house, hinnie, but I can give you my heart, my devotion, my enduring love, if you'll consent to becoming my wife."

All too aware of a score of people witnessing this proposal, Meg struggled for an appropriate response.

"Yes," someone hissed. "Just say yes."

"F–Father," Meg stammered.

"I have his blessing, if you can bear to be wed to a mere glassblower."

"Colin Grassick, I've never thought of you as a mere anything." Meg's tongue released with a spate of words. "How dare you think I would turn down the man I love because he works with his hands instead of ordering people about. Never has it been my choice to separate myself from people because—"

He raised his thumb from her chin to her lips, stilling the flow of speech. "Then I understand you are saying yes?"

"Yes!" Meg cried.

And as the Christmas party guests laughed and cheered, Colin lowered his head and kissed her in front of what sounded like half the residents of Salem County, New Jersey.

epilogue

Carriage wheels rumbled on the hard-packed lane leading to the Jordan house, and Colin grasped the railing around the porch to keep himself from jumping up and down like a small boy. Beside him Meg danced in place, sending her curls and hat ribbons bouncing.

"It's them, Colin, I know it is."

"Aye, lass, I believe so. But perhaps a wee bit of decorum before you meet my mother?" Grinning he tucked a pin back into her hair.

"Oh no, is she strict? You never told me she's strict."

"Nay, she's as gentle as a—well, she's more like a ewe than a lamb, but far smarter."

"She won't like me." Meg began fussing with her curls, her ribbons, the puffed sleeves of her muslin gown. "She'll take one look at me and say I'm not good enough for you. And she's right. You're so thoughtful and good, and I'm still willful and—oh, that cat!"

Wanderer rambled onto the porch, leaped atop the railing, and proceeded to bat at Meg's hat ribbons fluttering in the summer breeze.

"Leave her be, you beastie." Colin scooped the cat to the ground.

"Did he mess them up? Please make certain I look all right. I don't have time to go find a mirror."

"You look as bonnie as ever." Colin cupped her face in his hands and smiled into her eyes.

Behind her extraordinarily long lashes, the amber irises shimmered like gemstones. Her lips parted in a half smile, and he kissed them.

"Now they've come, we can wed, aye?"

"Aye, I mean, yes. Tomorrow. No, tomorrow is the Fourth of July. The day after. There they are."

"And none too soon."

Meg had refused to marry him until his family arrived. Sending messages to Scotland and making the arrangements for six Grassicks to pack up their home and sail across an ocean made hazardous by the war between England and France and uncomfortable relations with England and America, proved time-consuming and sometimes seemed impossible. But a messenger arrived on horseback the previous day announcing they would reach Salem County the next day.

That came, and there they were, five brothers and sisters tumbling from a coach, pushing and shoving, shrieking and crying, and looking like they'd grown a foot apiece.

Colin landed on the ground without use of the steps and raced forward to greet them. All of them at once. He gathered as many into his arms as he could reach and didn't mind that his eyes misted so badly he could scarcely see their faces.

"This country is huge."

"Are we going to live here?"

"Where can we go fishing?"

The questions poured over him, bombarded him, felt like a shower of gifts.

"And have you forgotten your mother, hinnie?" a soft voice asked from close beside him.

"I could never forget you." Colin drew her into the circle of his arms, too. "'Tis glad I am to have you here."

"And you." She stepped back and scanned him from head to toe. "America agrees with you."

"My bride-to-be takes good care of me." Colin glanced over his shoulder and saw Meg poised at the top of the steps, her fingers fluttering like her ribbons. "Will you come to meet them, Meg?"

She headed down the steps and glided over the gravel

with the grace of a princess. The children fell silent. The eldest of his brothers, a mere lad of eleven, stared with open admiration. The eldest girl, a woman of five and twenty, tilted her head to one side and pursed her lips then glanced down at her own muslin gown. She didn't need to speak for Colin to guess the comparisons she was making. If he knew his Meg, she would be giving Fiona and the other lasses half her gowns within the hour.

His Meg. The mere thought of that sent joy surging through him, and he stepped forward to take her hand in his. "Meg, let me present you to my mother and the rest of the clan; Fiona, Annabel, Jean, Jock, and Douglas."

"How do you do?" Her voice came out breathy, and her hand shook.

"Do not fash yourself over remembering all of them," Mother said, taking Meg's hand in both of hers. "Sometimes I forget them myself."

"How could you forget such beautiful children?" Meg glanced at Colin. "And you look too young to have a son as ancient as Colin."

Mother laughed. "I see you found yourself a flatterer."

"Oh no, I'm not like that. I'm simply on my best behavior today. I'm so afraid you'll meet me and not want me marrying your son and—"

"Hush, hinnie." Colin touched his finger to her lips. "They'll love you as much as I do soon enough."

"Indeed we will." Mother glanced from one of them to the other. "As long as you love my son and the Lord, you have my blessing."

"Well yes, I do, very much. And—oh, here's Father." She waved to Isaac as he exited the house. "Father, come meet Colin's family. Aren't they beautiful?"

"They are a fine sight to see in my yard." Meg's father descended the steps and held out his hand to Mother.

And as their hands and eyes met, Colin caught the flash of a bird taking flight, the bright yellow plumage of a goldfinch in full summer glory.

A Letter To Our Readers

Dear Reader:

In order that we might better contribute to your reading enjoyment, we would appreciate your taking a few minutes to respond to the following questions. We welcome your comments and read each form and letter we receive. When completed, please return to the following:

Fiction Editor
Heartsong Presents
PO Box 719
Uhrichsville, Ohio 44683

1. Did you enjoy reading *The Glassblower* by Laurie Alice Eakes?
   ❏ Very much! I would like to see more books by this author!
   ❏ Moderately. I would have enjoyed it more if

   _____
   _____
   _____

2. Are you a member of **Heartsong Presents**? ❏ Yes ❏ No
   If no, where did you purchase this book? _____
   _____

3. How would you rate, on a scale from 1 (poor) to 5 (superior), the cover design? _____

4. On a scale from 1 (poor) to 10 (superior), please rate the following elements.

   ____ Heroine   ____ Plot
   ____ Hero   ____ Inspirational theme
   ____ Setting   ____ Secondary characters

5. These characters were special because _____
_____
_____

6. How has this book inspired your life? _____
_____
_____

7. What settings would you like to see covered in future
   Heartsong Presents books? _____
_____
_____

8. What are some inspirational themes you would like to see
   treated in future books? _____
_____
_____

9. Would you be interested in reading other **Heartsong
   Presents** titles? ❑ Yes ❑ No

10. Please check your age range:
    ❑ Under 18   ❑ 18-24
    ❑ 25-34   ❑ 35-45
    ❑ 46-55   ❑ Over 55

Name _____
Occupation _____
Address _____
City, State, Zip _____
E-mail _____

THE BRIDE BLUNDER

A surprised groom sends for—and receives—the wrong bride in Kelly Eileen Hake's sequel to *The Bride Backfire*.

Historical, paperback, 288 pages, 5³/₁₆" x 8"